The Hidden Staircase

Both girls froze in their tracks

NANCY DREW MYSTERY STORIES

The Hidden Staircase

BY CAROLYN KEENE

Grosset & Dunlap
An Imprint of Penguin Group (USA) LLC

GROSSET & DUNLAP
Published by the Penguin Group
Penguin Group (USA) LLC, 375 Hudson Street, New York, New York 10014, USA

USA | Canada | UK | Ireland | Australia | New Zealand | India | South Africa | China

penguin.com
A Penguin Random House Company

Cover illustration by Sabrina Gabrielli.
Cover design by Mallory Grigg.

Library of Congress Cataloging-in-Publication Data is available.

ISBN 978-0-448-47970-5   10 9 8 7 6 5 4 3 2 1

Contents

CHAPTER I

The Haunted House

NANCY DREW began peeling off her garden gloves as she ran up the porch steps and into the hall to answer the ringing telephone. She picked it up and said, "Hello!"

"Hi, Nancy! This is Helen." Although Helen Corning was nearly three years older than Nancy, the two girls were close friends.

"Are you tied up on a case?" Helen asked.

"No. What's up? A mystery?"

"Yes—a haunted house."

Nancy sat down on the chair by the telephone. "Tell me more!" the eighteen-year-old detective begged excitedly.

"You've heard me speak of my Aunt Rosemary," Helen began. "Since becoming a widow, she has lived with her mother at Twin Elms, the old family mansion out in Cliffwood. Well, I went to see them yesterday. They said that many strange,

1

mysterious things have been happening there recently. I told them how good you are at solving
mysteries, and they'd like you to come out to Twin
Elms and help them." Helen paused, out of
breath.

"It certainly sounds intriguing," Nancy replied,
her eyes dancing.

"If you're not busy, Aunt Rosemary and I would
like to come over in about an hour and talk to you
about the ghost."

"I can't wait."

After Nancy had put down the phone, she sat
lost in thought for several minutes. Since solving
The Secret of the Old Clock, she had longed for
another case. Here was her chance!

Attractive, blond-haired Nancy was brought out
of her daydreaming by the sound of the doorbell.
At the same moment the Drews' housekeeper,
Hannah Gruen, came down the front stairs.

"I'll answer it," she offered.

Mrs. Gruen had lived with the Drews since
Nancy was three years old. At that time Mrs.
Drew had passed away and Hannah had become
like a second mother to Nancy. There was a deep
affection between the two, and Nancy confided all
her secrets to the understanding housekeeper.

Mrs. Gruen opened the door and instantly a
man stepped into the hall. He was short, thin,
and rather stooped. Nancy guessed his age to be
about forty.

"Is Mr. Drew at home?" he asked brusquely. "My name is Gomber—Nathan Gomber."

"No, he's not here just now," the housekeeper replied.

The caller looked over Hannah Gruen's shoulder and stared at Nancy. "Are you Nancy Drew?"

"Yes, I am. Is there anything I can do for you?"

The man's shifty gaze moved from Nancy to Hannah. "I've come out of the goodness of my heart to warn you and your father," he said pompously.

"Warn us? About what?" Nancy asked quickly.

Nathan Gomber straightened up importantly and said, "Your father is in great danger, Miss Drew!"

Both Nancy and Hannah Gruen gasped. "You mean this very minute?" the housekeeper questioned.

"All the time," was the startling answer. "I understand you're a pretty bright girl, Miss Drew —that you even solve mysteries. Well, right now I advise you to stick close to your father. Don't leave him for a minute."

Hannah Gruen looked as if she were ready to collapse and suggested that they all go into the living room, sit down, and talk the matter over. When they were seated, Nancy asked Nathan Gomber to explain further.

"The story in a nutshell is this," he began. "You know that your father was brought in to do legal work for the railroad when it was buying property for the new bridge here."

As Nancy nodded, he continued, "Well, a lot of the folks who sold their property think they were gypped."

Nancy's face reddened. "I understood from my father that everyone was well paid."

"That's not true," said Gomber. "Besides, the railroad is in a real mess now. One of the property owners, whose deed and signature they claim to have, says that he never signed the contract of sale."

"What's his name?" Nancy asked.

"Willie Wharton."

Nancy had not heard her father mention this name. She asked Gomber to go on with his story.

"I'm acting as agent for Willie Wharton and several of the land owners who were his neighbors," he said, "and they can make it pretty tough for the railroad. Willie Wharton's signature was never witnessed and the attached certificate of acknowledgment was not notarized. That's good proof the signature was a forgery. Well, if the railroad thinks they're going to get away with this, they're not!"

Nancy frowned. Such a procedure on the part of the property owners meant trouble for her father! She said evenly, "But all Willie Wharton has to do is swear before a notary that he did sign the contract of sale."

Gomber chuckled. "It's not that easy, Miss Drew. Willie Wharton is not available. Some of us have a good idea where he is and we'll produce him at the right time. But that time won't be until the railroad promises to give the sellers more money. Then he'll sign. You see, Willie is a real kind man and he wants to help his friends out whenever he can. Now he's got a chance."

Nancy had taken an instant dislike to Gomber and now it was quadrupled. She judged him to be the kind of person who stays within the boundaries of the law but whose ethics are questionable. This was indeed a tough problem for Mr. Drew!

"Who are the people who are apt to harm my father?" she asked.

"I'm not saying who they are," Nathan Gomber retorted. "You don't seem very appreciative of my coming here to warn you. Fine kind of a daughter you are. You don't care what happens to your father!"

Annoyed by the man's insolence, both Nancy and Mrs. Gruen angrily stood up. The housekeeper, pointing toward the front door, said, "Good day, Mr. Gomber!"

The caller shrugged as he too arose. "Have it your own way, but don't say I didn't warn you!"

He walked to the front door, opened it, and as he went outside, closed it with a tremendous bang.

"Well, of all the insulting people!" Hannah snorted.

Nancy nodded. "But that's not the worst of it, Hannah darling. I think there's more to Gomber's warning than he is telling. It seems to me to imply a threat. And he almost has me convinced. Maybe I should stay close to Dad until he and the other lawyers have straightened out this railroad tangle."

She said this would mean giving up a case she had been asked to take. Hastily Nancy gave Hannah the highlights of her conversation with Helen about the haunted mansion. "Helen and her aunt will be here in a little while to tell us the whole story."

"Oh, maybe things aren't so serious for your father as that horrible man made out," Hannah said encouragingly. "If I were you I'd listen to the details about the haunted house and then decide what you want to do about the mystery."

In a short time a sports car pulled into the winding, tree-shaded driveway of the Drew home. The large brick house was set some distance back from the street.

Helen was at the wheel and stopped just beyond the front entrance. She helped her aunt from the car and they came up the steps together. Mrs. Rosemary Hayes was tall and slender and had graying hair. Her face had a gentle expression but she looked tired.

Helen introduced her aunt to Nancy and to Hannah, and the group went into the living room to sit down. Hannah offered to prepare tea and left the room.

"Oh, Nancy," said Helen, "I do hope you can take Aunt Rosemary and Miss Flora's case." Quickly she explained that Miss Flora was her aunt's mother. "Aunt Rosemary is really my great-aunt and Miss Flora is my great-grandmother. From the time she was a little girl everybody has called her Miss Flora."

"The name may seem odd to people the first time they hear it," Mrs. Hayes remarked, "but we're all so used to it, we never think anything about it."

"Please tell me more about your house," Nancy requested, smiling.

"Mother and I are almost nervous wrecks," Mrs. Hayes replied. "I have urged her to leave Twin Elms, but she won't. You see, Mother has lived there ever since she married my father, Everett Turnbull."

Mrs. Hayes went on to say that all kinds of strange happenings had occurred during the past couple of weeks. They had heard untraceable music, thumps and creaking noises at night, and had seen eerie, indescribable shadows on walls.

"Have you notified the police?" Nancy asked.

"Oh, yes," Mrs. Hayes answered. "But after talking with my mother, they came to the conclusion that most of what she saw and heard could be explained by natural causes. The rest, they said, probably was imagination on her part. You see, she's over eighty years old, and while I know her mind is sound and alert, I'm afraid that the police don't think so."

After a pause Mrs. Hayes went on, "I had almost talked myself into thinking the ghostly noises could be attributed to natural causes, when something else happened."

"What was that?" Nancy questioned eagerly.

"We were robbed! During the night several pieces of old jewelry were taken. I did telephone the police about this and they came to the house for a description of the pieces. But they still would not admit that a 'ghost' visitor had taken them."

Nancy was thoughtful for several seconds before making a comment. Then she said, "Do the police have any idea who the thief might be?"

Aunt Rosemary shook her head. "No. And I'm afraid we might have more burglaries."

Many ideas were running through Nancy's head. One was that the thief apparently had no intention of harming anyone—that his only motive had been burglary. Was he or was he not the person who was "haunting" the house? Or could the strange happenings have some natural explanations, as the police had suggested?

At this moment Hannah returned with a large silver tray on which was a tea service and some dainty sandwiches. She set the tray on a table and asked Nancy to pour the tea. She herself passed the cups of tea and sandwiches to the callers.

As they ate, Helen said, "Aunt Rosemary hasn't told you half the things that have happened. Once Miss Flora thought she saw someone sliding out of a fireplace at midnight, and another time a chair moved from one side of the room to the other while her back was turned. But no one was there!"

"How extraordinary!" Hannah Gruen exclaimed. "I've often read about such things, but I never thought I'd meet anyone who lived in a haunted house."

Helen turned to Nancy and gazed pleadingly at her friend. "You see how much you're needed at Twin Elms? Won't you please go out there with me and solve the mystery of the ghost?"

CHAPTER II

The Mysterious Mishap

SIPPING their tea, Helen Corning and her aunt waited for Nancy's decision. The young sleuth was in a dilemma. She wanted to start at once solving the mystery of the "ghost" of Twin Elms. But Nathan Gomber's warning still rang in her ears and she felt that her first duty was to stay with her father.

At last she spoke. "Mrs. Hayes—" she began.

"Please call me Aunt Rosemary," the caller requested. "All Helen's friends do."

Nancy smiled. "I'd love to. Aunt Rosemary, may I please let you know tonight or tomorrow? I really must speak to my father about the case. And something else came up just this afternoon which may keep me at home for a while at least."

"I understand," Mrs. Hayes answered, trying to conceal her disappointment.

Helen Corning did not take Nancy's announcement so calmly. "Oh, Nancy, you just must come. I'm sure your dad would want you to help us. Can't you postpone the other thing until you get back?"

"I'm afraid not," said Nancy. "I can't tell you all the details, but Dad has been threatened and I feel that I ought to stay close to him."

Hannah Gruen added her fears. "Goodness only knows what they may do to Mr. Drew," she said. "Somebody could come up and hit him on the head, or poison his food in a restaurant, or—"

Helen and her aunt gasped. "It's that bad?" Helen asked, her eyes growing wide.

Nancy explained that she would talk to her father when he returned home. "I hate to disappoint you," she said, "but you can see what a quandary I'm in."

"You poor girl!" said Mrs. Hayes sympathetically. "Now don't you worry about us."

Nancy smiled. "I'll worry whether I come or not," she said. "Anyway, I'll talk to my dad tonight."

The callers left shortly. When the door had closed behind them, Hannah put an arm around Nancy's shoulders. "I'm sure everything will come out all right for everybody," she said. "I'm sorry I talked about those dreadful things that might happen to your father. I let my imagination run away with me, just like they say Miss Flora's does with her."

"You're a great comfort, Hannah dear," said Nancy. "To tell the truth, I have thought of all kinds of horrible things myself." She began to pace the floor. "I wish Dad would get home."

During the next hour she went to the window at least a dozen times, hoping to see her father's car coming up the street. It was not until six o'clock that she heard the crunch of wheels on the driveway and saw Mr. Drew's sedan pull into the garage.

"He's safe!" she cried out to Hannah, who was testing potatoes that were baking in the oven.

In a flash Nancy was out the back door and running to meet her father. "Oh, Dad, I'm so glad to see you!" she exclaimed.

She gave him a tremendous hug and a resounding kiss. He responded affectionately, but gave a little chuckle. "What have I done to rate this extra bit of attention?" he teased. With a wink he added, "I know. Your date for tonight is off and you want me to substitute."

"Oh, Dad," Nancy replied. "Of course my date's not off. But I'm just about to call it off."

"Why?" Mr. Drew questioned. "Isn't Dirk going to stay on your list?"

"It's not that," Nancy replied. "It's because— because you're in terrible danger, Dad. I've been warned not to leave you."

Instead of looking alarmed, the lawyer burst out laughing. "In terrible danger of what? Are you going to make a raid on my wallet?"

"Dad, be serious! I really mean what I'm saying. Nathan Gomber was here and told me that you're in great danger and I'd better stay with you at all times."

The lawyer sobered at once. "That pest again!" he exclaimed. "There are times when I'd like to thrash the man till he begged for mercy!"

Mr. Drew suggested that they postpone their discussion about Nathan Gomber until dinner was over. Then he would tell his daughter the true facts in the case. After they had finished dinner, Hannah insisted upon tidying up alone while father and daughter talked.

"I will admit that there is a bit of a muddle about the railroad bridge," Mr. Drew began. "What happened was that the lawyer who went to get Willie Wharton's signature was very ill at the time. Unfortunately, he failed to have the signature witnessed or have the attached certificate of acknowledgment executed. The poor man passed away a few hours later."

"And the other railroad lawyers failed to notice that the signature hadn't been witnessed or the certificate notarized?" Nancy asked.

"Not right away. The matter did not come to light until the man's widow turned his brief case over to the railroad. The old deed to Wharton's property was there, so the lawyers assumed that the signature on the contract was genuine. The contract for the railroad bridge was awarded and

work began. Suddenly Nathan Gomber appeared,
saying he represented Willie Wharton and others
who had owned property which the railroad had
bought on either side of the Muskoka River."

"I understood from Mr. Gomber," said Nancy,
"that Willie Wharton is trying to get more money
for his neighbors by holding out for a higher price
himself."

"That's the story. Personally, I think it's a
sharp deal on Gomber's part. The more people
he can get money for, the higher his commission,"
Mr. Drew stated.

"What a mess!" Nancy exclaimed. "And what
can be done?"

"To tell the truth, there is little anyone can do
until Willie Wharton is found. Gomber knows
this, of course, and has probably advised Wharton
to stay in hiding until the railroad agrees to give
everybody more money."

Nancy had been watching her father intently.
Now she saw an expression of eagerness come over
his face. He leaned forward in his chair and said,
"But I think I'm about to outwit Mr. Nathan
Gomber. I've had a tip that Willie Wharton is
in Chicago and I'm leaving Monday morning to
find out."

Mr. Drew went on, "I believe that Wharton will
say he did sign the contract of sale which the railroad company has and will readily consent to having the certificate of acknowledgment notarized.

Then, of course, the railroad won't pay him or any of the other property owners another cent."

"But, Dad, you still haven't convinced me you're not in danger," Nancy reminded him.

"Nancy dear," her father replied, "I feel that I am not in danger. Gomber is nothing but a blowhard. I doubt that he or Willie Wharton or any of the other property owners would resort to violence to keep me from working on this case. He's just trying to scare me into persuading the railroad to accede to his demands."

Nancy looked skeptical. "But don't forget that you're about to go to Chicago and produce the very man Gomber and those property owners don't want around here just now."

"I know." Mr. Drew nodded. "But I still doubt if anyone would use force to keep me from going." Laughingly the lawyer added, "So I won't need you as a bodyguard, Nancy."

His daughter gave a sigh of resignation. "All right, Dad, you know best." She then proceeded to tell her father about the Twin Elms mystery, which she had been asked to solve. "If you approve," Nancy said in conclusion, "I'd like to go over there with Helen."

Mr. Drew had listened with great interest. Now, after a few moments of thought, he smiled. "Go by all means, Nancy. I realize you've been itching to work on a new case—and this sounds like a real challenge. But please be careful."

"Oh, I will, Dad!" Nancy promised, her face lighting up. "Thanks a million." She jumped from her chair, gave her father a kiss, then went to phone Helen the good news. It was arranged that the girls would go to Twin Elms on Monday morning.

Nancy returned to the living room, eager to discuss the mystery further. Her father, however, glanced at his wrist watch. "Say, young lady, you'd better go dress for that date of yours." He winked. "I happen to know that Dirk doesn't like to be kept waiting."

"Especially by any of my mysteries." She laughed and hurried upstairs to change into a dance dress.

Half an hour later Dirk Jackson arrived. Nancy and the red-haired, former high-school tennis champion drove off to pick up another couple and attend an amateur play and dance given by the local Little Theater group.

Nancy thoroughly enjoyed herself and was sorry when the affair ended. With the promise of another date as soon as she returned from Twin Elms, Nancy said good night and waved from her doorway to the departing boy. As she prepared for bed, she thought of the play, the excellent orchestra, how lucky she was to have Dirk for a date, and what fun it had all been. But then her thoughts turned to Helen Corning and her relatives in the haunted house, Twin Elms.

"I can hardly wait for Monday to come," she murmured to herself as she fell asleep.

The following morning she and her father attended church together. Hannah said she was going to a special service that afternoon and therefore would stay at home during the morning.

"I'll have a good dinner waiting for you," she announced, as the Drews left.

After the service was over, Mr. Drew said he would like to drive down to the waterfront and see what progress had been made on the new bridge. "The railroad is going ahead with construction on the far side of the river," he told Nancy.

"Is the Wharton property on this side?" Nancy asked.

"Yes. And I must get to the truth of this mixed-up situation, so that work can be started on this side too."

Mr. Drew wound among the many streets leading down to the Muskoka River, then took the vehicular bridge across. He turned toward the construction area and presently parked his car. As he and Nancy stepped from the sedan, he looked ruefully at her pumps.

"It's going to be rough walking down to the waterfront," he said. "Perhaps you had better wait here."

"Oh, I'll be all right," Nancy assured him. "I'd like to see what's being done."

Various pieces of large machinery stood about on the high ground—a crane, a derrick, and hydraulic shovels. As the Drews walked toward the river, they passed a large truck. It faced the river and stood at the top of an incline just above two of the four enormous concrete piers which had already been built.

"I suppose there will be matching piers on the opposite side," Nancy mused, as she and her father reached the riverbank. They paused in the space between the two huge abutments. Mr. Drew glanced from side to side as if he had heard something. Suddenly Nancy detected a noise behind them.

Turning, she was horrified to see that the big truck was moving toward them. No one was at the wheel and the great vehicle was gathering speed at every moment.

"Dad!" she screamed.

In the brief second of warning, the truck almost seemed to leap toward the water. Nancy and her father, hemmed in by the concrete piers, had no way to escape being run down.

"Dive!" Mr. Drew ordered.

Without hesitation, he and Nancy made running flat dives into the water, and with arms flailing and legs kicking, swam furiously out of harm's way.

The truck thundered into the water and sank

The truck seemed to leap toward them

immediately up to the cab. The Drews turned and came back to the shore.

"Whew! That was a narrow escape!" the lawyer exclaimed, as he helped his daughter retrieve her pumps which had come off in the oozy bank.

"And what sights we are!" Nancy remarked.

"Indeed we are," her father agreed, as they trudged up the incline. "I'd like to get hold of the workman who was careless enough to leave that heavy truck on the slope without the brake on properly."

Nancy was not so sure that the near accident was the fault of a careless workman. Nathan Gomber had warned her that Mr. Drew's life was in danger. The threat might already have been put into action!

CHAPTER III

A Stolen Necklace

"WE'D better get home in a hurry and change our clothes," said Mr. Drew. "And I'll call the contracting company to tell them what happened."

"And notify the police?" Nancy suggested.

She dropped behind her father and gazed over the surrounding ground for telltale footprints. Presently she saw several at the edge of the spot where the truck had stood.

"Dad!" the young sleuth called out. "I may have found a clue to explain how that truck started downhill."

Her father came back and looked at the footprints. They definitely had not been made by a workman's boots.

"You may think me an old worrier, Dad," Nancy spoke up, "but these footprints, made by a man's business shoes, convince me that somebody deliberately tried to injure us with that truck."

The lawyer stared at his daughter. Then he looked down at the ground. From the size of the shoe and the length of the stride one could easily perceive that the wearer of the shoes was not tall. Nancy asked her father if he thought one of the workmen on the project could be responsible.

"I just can't believe anyone associated with the contracting company would want to injure us," Mr. Drew said.

Nancy reminded her father of Nathan Gomber's warning. "It might be one of the property owners, or even Willie Wharton himself."

"Wharton is short and has a small foot," the lawyer conceded. "And I must admit that these look like fresh footprints. As a matter of fact, they show that whoever was here ran off in a hurry. He may have released the brake on the truck, then jumped out and run away."

"Yes," said Nancy. "And that means the attack *was* deliberate."

Mr. Drew did not reply. He continued walking up the hill, lost in thought. Nancy followed and they climbed into the car. They drove home in silence, each puzzling over the strange incident of the runaway truck. Upon reaching the house, they were greeted by a loud exclamation of astonishment.

"My goodness!" Hannah Gruen cried out. "Whatever in the world happened to you?"

They explained hastily, then hurried upstairs

to bathe and change into dry clothes. By the time they reached the first floor again, Hannah had placed sherbet glasses filled with orange and grapefruit slices on the table. All during the delicious dinner of spring lamb, rice and mushrooms, fresh peas and chocolate angel cake with vanilla ice cream, the conversation revolved around the railroad bridge mystery and then the haunted Twin Elms mansion.

"I knew things wouldn't be quiet around here for long," Hannah Gruen remarked with a smile. "Tomorrow you'll both be off on big adventures. I certainly wish you both success."

"Thank you, Hannah," said Nancy. She laughed. "I'd better get a good night's sleep. From now on I may be kept awake by ghosts and strange noises."

"I'm a little uneasy about your going to Twin Elms," the housekeeper told her. "Please promise me that you'll be careful."

"Of course," Nancy replied. Turning to her father, she said, "Pretend I've said the same thing to you about being careful."

The lawyer chuckled and pounded his chest. "You know me. I can be pretty tough when the need arises."

Early the next morning Nancy drove her father to the airport in her blue convertible. Just before she kissed him good-by at the turnstile, he said, "I expect to return on Wednesday, Nancy. Suppose

I stop off at Cliffwood and see how you're making out?"

"Wonderful, Dad! I'll be looking for you."

As soon as her father left, Nancy drove directly to Helen Corning's home. The pretty, brunette girl came from the front door of the white cottage, swinging a suitcase. She tossed it into the rear of Nancy's convertible and climbed in.

"I ought to be scared," said Helen. "Goodness only knows what's ahead of us. But right now I'm so happy nothing could upset me."

"What happened?" Nancy asked as she started the car. "Did you inherit a million?"

"Something better than that," Helen replied. "Nancy, I want to tell you a big, big secret. I'm going to be married!"

Nancy slowed the car and pulled to the side of the street. Leaning over to hug her friend, she said, "Why, Helen, how wonderful! Who is he? And tell me all about it. This is rather sudden, isn't it?"

"Yes, it is," Helen confessed. "His name is Jim Archer and he's simply out of this world. I'm a pretty lucky girl. I met him a couple of months ago when he was home on a short vacation. He works for the Tristam Oil Company and has spent two years abroad. Jim will be away a while longer, and then be given a position here in the States."

As Nancy started the car up once more, her eyes

twinkled. "Helen Corning, have you been engaged for two months and didn't tell me?"

Helen shook her head. "Jim and I have been corresponding ever since he left. Last night he telephoned from overseas and asked me to marry him." Helen giggled. "I said yes in a big hurry. Then he asked to speak to Dad. My father gave his consent but insisted that our engagement not be announced until Jim's return to this country."

The two girls discussed all sorts of delightful plans for Helen's wedding and before they knew it they had reached the town of Cliffwood.

"My great-grandmother's estate is about two miles out of town," Helen said. "Go down Main Street and turn right at the fork."

Ten minutes later she pointed out Twin Elms. From the road one could see little of the house. A high stone wall ran along the front of the estate and beyond it were many tall trees. Nancy turned into the driveway which twisted and wound among elms, oaks, and maples.

Presently the old Colonial home came into view. Helen said it had been built in 1785 and had been given its name because of the two elm trees which stood at opposite ends of the long building. They had grown to be giants and their foliage was beautiful. The mansion was of red brick and nearly all the walls were covered with ivy. There was a ten-foot porch with tall white pillars at the huge front door.

"It's charming!" Nancy commented as she pulled up to the porch.

"Wait until you see the grounds," said Helen. "There are several old, old buildings. An icehouse, a smokehouse, a kitchen, and servants' cottages."

"The mansion certainly doesn't look spooky from the outside," Nancy commented.

At that moment the great door opened and Aunt Rosemary came outside. "Hello, girls," she greeted them. "I'm so glad to see you."

Nancy felt the warmness of the welcome but thought that it was tinged with worry. She wondered if another "ghost" incident had taken place at the mansion.

The girls took their suitcases from the car and followed Mrs. Hayes inside. Although the furnishings looked rather worn, they were still very beautiful. The high-ceilinged rooms opened off a center hall and in a quick glance Nancy saw lovely damask draperies, satin-covered sofas and chairs, and on the walls, family portraits in large gilt frames of scrollwork design.

Aunt Rosemary went to the foot of the shabbily carpeted stairway, took hold of the handsome mahogany balustrade, and called, "Mother, the girls are here!"

In a moment a slender, frail-looking woman with snow-white hair started to descend the steps. Her face, though older in appearance than Rosemary's, had the same gentle smile. As Miss Flora reached the foot of the stairs, she held out her hands to both girls.

At once Helen said, "I'd like to present Nancy Drew, Miss Flora."

"I'm so glad you could come, my dear," the elderly woman said. "I know that you're going to solve this mystery which has been bothering Rosemary and me. I'm sorry not to be able to entertain you more auspiciously, but a haunted house hardly lends itself to gaiety."

The dainty, yet stately, Miss Flora swept toward a room which she referred to as the parlor. It was opposite the library. She sat down in a high-backed chair and asked everyone else to be seated.

"Mother," said Aunt Rosemary, "we don't have to be so formal with Nancy and Helen. I'm sure they'll understand that we've just been badly frightened." She turned toward the girls. "Something happened a little while ago that has made us very jittery."

"Yes," Miss Flora said. "A pearl necklace of mine was stolen!"

"You don't mean the lovely one that has been in the family so many years!" Helen cried out.

The two women nodded. Then Miss Flora said, "Oh, I probably was very foolish. It's my own fault. While I was in my room, I took the necklace from the hiding place where I usually keep it. The catch had not worked well the last

time I wore the pearls and I wanted to examine it.
While I was doing this, Rosemary called to me to
come downstairs. The gardener was here and
wanted to talk about some work. I put the necklace in my dresser drawer. When I returned ten
minutes later the necklace wasn't there!"

"How dreadful!" said Nancy sympathetically.
"Had anybody come into the house during that
time?"

"Not to our knowledge," Aunt Rosemary replied. "Ever since we've had this ghost visiting us
we've kept every door and window on the first
floor locked all the time."

Nancy asked if the two women had gone out into
the garden to speak to their helper. "Mother
did," said Mrs. Hayes. "But I was in the kitchen
the entire time. If anyone came in the back door,
I certainly would have seen the person."

"Is there a back stairway to the second floor?"
Nancy asked.

"Yes," Miss Flora answered. "But there are
doors at both top and bottom and we keep them
locked. No one could have gone up that way."

"Then anyone who came into the house had to
go up by way of the front stairs?"

"Yes." Aunt Rosemary smiled a little. "But if
anyone had, I would have noticed. You probably
heard how those stairs creak when Mother came
down. This can be avoided if you hug the wall,
but practically no one knows that."

"May I go upstairs and look around?" Nancy questioned.

"Of course, dear. And I'll show you and Helen to your room," Aunt Rosemary said.

The girls picked up their suitcases and followed the two women up the stairs. Nancy and Helen were given a large, quaint room at the front of the old house over the library. They quickly deposited their luggage, then Miss Flora led the way across the hall to her room, which was directly above the parlor. It was large and very attractive with its canopied mahogany bed and an old-fashioned candlewick spread. The dresser, dressing table, and chairs also were mahogany. Long chintz draperies hung at the windows.

An eerie feeling began to take possession of Nancy. She could almost feel the presence of a ghostly burglar on the premises. Though she tried to shake off the mood, it persisted. Finally she told herself that it was possible the thief was still around. If so, he must be hiding.

Against one wall stood a large walnut wardrobe. Helen saw Nancy gazing at it intently. She went over and whispered, "Do you think there might be someone inside?"

"Who knows?" Nancy replied in a low voice. "Let's find out!"

She walked across the room, and taking hold of the two knobs on the double doors, opened them wide.

CHAPTER IV

Strange Music

THE ANXIOUS group stared inside the wardrobe. No one stood there. Dresses, suits, and coats hung in an orderly row.

Nancy took a step forward and began separating them. Someone, she thought, might be hiding behind the clothes. The others in the room held their breaths as she made a thorough search.

"No one here!" she finally announced, and a sigh of relief escaped the lips of Miss Flora and Aunt Rosemary.

The young sleuth said she would like to make a thorough inspection of all possible hiding places on the second floor. With Helen helping her, they went from room to room, opening wardrobe doors and looking under beds. They did not find the thief.

Nancy suggested that Miss Flora and Aunt Rose-

mary report the theft to the police, but the older
woman shook her head. Mrs. Hayes, although she
agreed this might be wise, added softly, "Mother
just *might* be mistaken. She's a little forgetful at
times about where she puts things."

With this possibility in mind, she and the girls
looked in every drawer in the room, under the
mattress and pillows, and even in the pockets of
Miss Flora's clothes. The pearl necklace was not
found. Nancy suggested that she and Helen try
to find out how the thief had made his entrance.

Helen led the way outdoors. At once Nancy
began to look for footprints. No tracks were visible on the front or back porches, or on any of the
walks, which were made of finely crushed stone.

"We'll look in the soft earth beneath the windows," Nancy said. "Maybe the thief climbed in."

"But Aunt Rosemary said all the windows on
the first floor are kept locked," Helen objected.

"No doubt," Nancy said. "But I think we
should look for footprints just the same."

The girls went from window to window, but
there were no footprints beneath any. Finally
Nancy stopped and looked thoughtfully at the ivy
on the walls.

"Do you think the thief climbed up to the second floor that way?" Helen asked her. "But
there'd still be footprints on the ground."

Nancy said that the thief could have carried a
plank with him, laid it down, and stepped from the

walk to the wall of the house. "Then he could have climbed up the ivy and down again, and gotten back to the walk without leaving any footprints."

Once more Nancy went around the entire house, examining every bit of ivy which wound up from the foundation. Finally she said, "No, the thief didn't get into the house this way."

"Well, he certainly didn't fly in," said Helen. "So *how* did he enter?"

Nancy laughed. "If I could tell you that I'd have the mystery half solved."

She said that she would like to look around the grounds of Twin Elms. "It may give us a clue as to how the thief got into the house."

As they strolled along, Nancy kept a sharp lookout but saw nothing suspicious. At last they came to a half-crumbled brick walk laid out in an interesting crisscross pattern.

"Where does this walk lead?" Nancy asked.

"Well, I guess originally it went over to Riverview Manor, the next property," Helen replied. "I'll show you that mansion later. The first owner was a brother of the man who built this place."

Helen went on to say that Riverview Manor was a duplicate of Twin Elms mansion. The two brothers had been inseparable companions, but their sons who later lived there had had a violent quarrel and had become lifelong enemies.

"Riverview Manor has been sold several times during the years but has been vacant for a long time."

"You mean no one lives there now?" Nancy asked. As Helen nodded, she added with a laugh, "Then maybe that's the ghost's home!"

"In that case he really must be a ghost," said Helen lightly. "There's not a piece of furniture in the house."

The two girls returned to the Twin Elms mansion and reported their lack of success in picking up a clue to the intruder. Nancy, recalling that many Colonial houses had secret entrances and passageways, asked Miss Flora, "Do you know of any secret entrance to your home that the thief could use?"

She said no, and explained that her husband had been a rather reticent person and had passed away when Rosemary was only a baby. "It's just possible he knew of a secret entrance, but did not want to worry me by telling me about it," Mrs. Turnbull said.

Aunt Rosemary, sensing that her mother was becoming alarmed by the questions, suggested that they all have lunch. The two girls went with her to the kitchen and helped prepare a tasty meal of chicken salad, biscuits, and fruit gelatin.

During the meal the conversation covered several subjects, but always came back to the topic of the mystery. They had just finished eating when suddenly Nancy sat straight up in her chair.

"What's the matter?" Helen asked her.

Nancy was staring out the dining-room door to-ward the stairway in the hall. Then she turned to Miss Flora. "Did you leave a radio on in your bedroom?"

"Why, no."

"Did you, Aunt Rosemary?"

"No. Neither Mother nor I turned our radios on this morning. Why do—" She stopped speaking, for now all of them could distinctly hear music coming from the second floor.

Helen and Nancy were out of their chairs in-stantly. They dashed into the hall and up the stairway. The music was coming from Miss Flora's room, and when the girls rushed in, they knew indeed that it was from her radio.

Nancy went over to examine the set. It was an old one and did not have a clock attachment with an automatic control.

"Someone came into this room and turned on the radio!" she stated.

A look of alarm came over Helen's face, but she tried to shake off her nervousness and asked, "Nancy, do you think the radio could have been turned on by remote control? I've heard of such things."

Nancy said she doubted this. "I'm afraid, Helen, that the thief has been in the house all the time. He and the ghost are one and the same person. Oh, I wish we had looked before in the cellar and the attic. Maybe it's not too late. Come on!"

Helen, instead of moving from the room, stared at the fireplace. "Nancy," she said, "do you suppose someone is hiding up there?"

Without hesitation she crossed the room, got down on her knees, and tried to look up the chimney. The damper was closed. Reaching her arm up, Helen pulled the handle to open it.

The next moment she cried out, "Ugh!"

"Oh, Helen, you poor thing!" Nancy exclaimed, running to her friend's side.

A shower of soot had come down, covering Helen's hair, face, shoulders, and arms.

"Get me a towel, will you, Nancy?" she requested.

Nancy dashed to the bathroom and grabbed two large towels. She wrapped them around her friend, then went with Helen to help her with a shampoo and general cleanup job. Finally Nancy brought her another sports dress.

"I guess my idea about chimneys wasn't so good," Helen stated ruefully. "And we're probably too late to catch the thief."

Nevertheless, she and Nancy climbed the stairs to the attic and looked behind trunks and boxes to see if anyone were hiding. Next, the girls went to the cellar and inspected the various rooms there. Still there was no sign of the thief who had entered Twin Elms.

After Miss Flora had heard the whole story, she gave a nervous sigh. "It's the ghost—there's no other explanation."

"But why," Aunt Rosemary asked, "has a ghost suddenly started performing here? This house has been occupied since 1785 and no ghost was ever reported haunting the place."

"Well, apparently robbery is the motive," Nancy replied. "But why the thief bothers to frighten you is something I haven't figured out yet."

"The main thing," Helen spoke up, "is to catch him!"

"Oh, if we only could!" Miss Flora said, her voice a bit shaky.

The girls were about to pick up the luncheon dishes from the table, to carry them to the kitchen, when the front door knocker sounded loudly.

"Oh, dear," said Miss Flora, "who can that be? Maybe it's the thief and he's come to harm us!"

Aunt Rosemary put an arm around her mother's shoulders. "Please don't worry," she begged. "I think our caller is probably the man who wants to buy Twin Elms." She turned to Nancy and Helen. "But Mother doesn't want to sell for the low price that he is offering."

Nancy said she would go to the door. She set the dishes down and walked out to the hall. Reaching the great door, she flung it open.

Nathan Gomber stood there!

CHAPTER V

A Puzzling Interview

FOR SEVERAL seconds Nathan Gomber stared at Nancy in disbelief. "You!" he cried out finally.

"You didn't expect to find me here, did you?" she asked coolly.

"I certainly didn't. I thought you'd taken my advice and stayed with your father. Young people today are so hardhearted!" Gomber wagged his head in disgust.

Nancy ignored Gomber's remarks. Shrugging, the man pushed his way into the hall. "I know this. If anything happens to your father, you'll never forgive yourself. But you can't blame Nathan Gomber! I warned you!"

Still Nancy made no reply. She kept looking at him steadily, trying to figure out what was really in his mind. She was convinced it was not solicitude for her father.

Nathan Gomber changed the subject abruptly.

"I'd like to see Mrs. Turnbull and Mrs. Hayes," he said. "Go call them."

Nancy was annoyed by Gomber's crudeness, but she turned around and went down the hall to the dining room.

"We heard every word," Miss Flora said in a whisper. "I shan't see Mr. Gomber. I don't want to sell this house."

Nancy was amazed to hear this. "You mean he's the person who wants to buy it?"

"Yes."

Instantly Nancy was on the alert. Because of the nature of the railroad deal in which Nathan Gomber was involved, she was distrustful of his motives in wanting to buy Twin Elms. It flashed through her mind that perhaps he was trying to buy it at a very low price and planned to sell it off in building lots at a huge profit.

"Suppose I go tell him you don't want to sell," Nancy suggested in a low voice.

But her caution was futile. Hearing footsteps behind her, she turned to see Gomber standing in the doorway.

"Howdy, everybody!" he said.

Miss Flora, Aunt Rosemary, and Helen showed annoyance. It was plain that all of them thought the man completely lacking in good manners.

Aunt Rosemary's jaw was set in a grim line, but she said politely, "Helen, this is Mr. Gomber. Mr. Gomber, my niece, Miss Corning."

"Pleased to meet you," said their caller, extending a hand to shake Helen's.

"Nancy, I guess you've met Mr. Gomber," Aunt Rosemary went on.

"Oh, sure!" Nathan Gomber said with a somewhat raucous laugh. "Nancy and me, we've met!"

"Only once," Nancy said pointedly.

Ignoring her rebuff, he went on, "Nancy Drew is a very strange young lady. Her father's in great danger and I tried to warn her to stick close to him. Instead of that, she's out here visiting you folks."

"Her father's in danger?" Miss Flora said worriedly.

"Dad says he's not," Nancy replied. "And besides, I'm sure my father would know how to take care of any enemies." She looked straight at Nathan Gomber, as if to let him know that the Drews were not easily frightened.

"Well," the caller said, "let's get down to business." He pulled an envelope full of papers from his pocket. "Everything's here—all ready for you to sign, Mrs. Turnbull."

"I don't wish to sell at such a low figure," Miss Flora told him firmly. "In fact, I don't know that I want to sell at all."

Nathan Gomber tossed his head. "You'll sell all right," he prophesied. "I've been talking to some of the folks downtown. Everybody knows this old place is haunted and nobody would give you five cents for it—that is, nobody but me."

As he waited for his words to sink in, Nancy spoke up, "If the house is haunted, why do you want it?"

"Well," Gomber answered, "I guess I'm a gambler at heart. I'd be willing to put some money into this place, even if there is a ghost parading around." He laughed loudly, then went on, "I declare it might be a real pleasure to meet a ghost and get the better of it!"

Nancy thought with disgust, "Nathan Gomber, you're about the most conceited, obnoxious person I've met in a long time."

Suddenly the expression of cunning on the man's face changed completely. An almost wistful look came into his eyes. He sat down on one of the dining-room chairs and rested his chin in his hand.

"I guess you think I'm just a hardheaded business man with no feelings," he said. "The truth is I'm a real softy. I'll tell you why I want this old house so bad. I've always dreamed of owning a Colonial mansion, and having a kinship with early America. You see, my family were poor folks in Europe. Now that I've made a little money, I'd like to have a home like this to roam around in and enjoy its traditions."

Miss Flora seemed to be touched by Gomber's story. "I had no idea you wanted the place so much," she said kindly. "Maybe I ought to give it up. It's really too big for us."

As Aunt Rosemary saw her mother weakening, she said quickly, "You don't have to sell this house, Mother. You know you love it. So far as the ghost is concerned, I'm sure that mystery is going to be cleared up. Then you'd be sorry you had parted with Twin Elms. Please don't say yes!"

As Gomber gave Mrs. Hayes a dark look, Nancy asked him, "Why don't you buy Riverview Manor? It's a duplicate of this place and is for sale. You probably could purchase it at a lower price than you could this one."

"I've seen that place," the man returned. "It's in a bad state. It would cost me a mint of money to fix it up. No sir. I want this place and I'm going to have it!"

This bold remark was too much for Aunt Rosemary. Her eyes blazing, she said, "Mr. Gomber, this interview is at an end. Good-by!"

To Nancy's delight and somewhat to her amusement, Nathan Gomber obeyed the "order" to leave. He seemed to be almost meek as he walked through the hall and let himself out the front door.

"Of all the nerve!" Helen burst out.

"Perhaps we shouldn't be too hard on the man," Miss Flora said timidly. "His story is a pathetic one and I can see how he might want to pretend he had an old American family background."

"I'd like to bet a cooky Mr. Gomber didn't mean one word of what he was saying," Helen remarked.

"Oh dear, I'm so confused," said Miss Flora, her voice trembling. "Let's all sit down in the parlor and talk about it a little more."

The two girls stepped back as Miss Flora, then Aunt Rosemary, left the dining room. They followed to the parlor and sat down together on the recessed couch by the fireplace. Nancy, on a sudden hunch, ran to a front window to see which direction Gomber had taken. To her surprise he was walking down the winding driveway.

"That's strange. Evidently he didn't drive," Nancy told herself. "It's quite a walk into town to get a train or bus to River Heights."

As Nancy mulled over this idea, trying to figure out the answer, she became conscious of creaking sounds. Helen suddenly gave a shriek. Nancy turned quickly.

"Look!" Helen cried, pointing toward the ceiling, and everyone stared upward.

The crystal chandelier had suddenly started swaying from side to side!

"The ghost again!" Miss Flora cried out. She looked as if she were about to faint.

Nancy's eyes quickly swept the room. Nothing else in it was moving, so vibration was not causing the chandelier to sway. As it swung back and forth, a sudden thought came to the young sleuth. Maybe someone in Miss Flora's room above was causing the shaking.

The chandelier suddenly started to sway

"I'm going upstairs to investigate," Nancy told the others.

Racing noiselessly on tiptoe out of the room and through the hall, she began climbing the stairs, hugging the wall so the steps would not creak. As she neared the top, Nancy was sure she heard a door close. Hurrying along the hall, she burst into Miss Flora's bedroom. No one was in sight!

"Maybe this time the ghost couldn't get away and is in that wardrobe!" Nancy thought.

Helen and her relatives had come up the stairs behind Nancy. They reached the bedroom just as she flung open the wardrobe doors. But for the second time she found no one hiding there.

Nancy bit her lip in vexation. The ghost was clever indeed. Where *had* he gone? She had given him no time to go down the hall or run into another room. Yet there was no denying the fact that he had been in Miss Flora's room!

"Tell us why you came up," Helen begged her. Nancy told her theory, but suddenly she realized that maybe she was letting her imagination run wild. It was possible, she admitted to the others, that no one had caused the chandelier to shake.

"There's only one way to find out," she said. "I'll make a test."

Nancy asked Helen to go back to the first floor and watch the chandelier. She would try to make it sway by rocking from side to side on the floor above it.

"If this works, then I'm sure we've picked up a clue to the ghost," she said hopefully.

Helen readily agreed and left the room. When Nancy thought her friend had had time to reach the parlor below, she began to rock hard from side to side on the spot above the chandelier.

She had barely started the test when from the first floor Helen Corning gave a piercing scream!

CHAPTER VI

The Gorilla Face

"SOMETHING has happened to Helen!" Aunt Rosemary cried out fearfully.

Nancy was already racing through the second-floor hallway. Reaching the stairs, she leaped down them two steps at a time. Helen Corning had collapsed in a wing chair in the parlor, her hands over her face.

"Helen! What happened?" Nancy asked, reaching her friend's side.

"Out there! Looking in that window!" Helen pointed to the front window of the parlor next to the hall. "The most horrible face I ever saw!"

"Was it a man's face?" Nancy questioned.

"Oh, I don't know. It looked just like a gorilla!" Helen closed her eyes as if to shut out the memory of the sight.

Nancy did not wait to hear any more. In another second she was at the front door and had yanked it open. Stepping outside, she looked all around. She could see no animal near the house, nor any sign under the window that one had stood there.

Puzzled, the young sleuth hurried down the steps and began a search of the grounds. By this time Helen had collected her wits and come outside. She joined Nancy and together they looked in every outbuilding and behind every clump of bushes on the grounds of Twin Elms. They did not find one footprint or any other evidence to prove that a gorilla or other creature had been on the grounds of the estate.

"I saw it! I know I saw it!" Helen insisted.

"I don't doubt you," Nancy replied.

"Then what explanation is there?" Helen demanded. "You know I never did believe in spooks. But if we have many more of these weird happenings around here, I declare I'm going to start believing in ghosts."

Nancy laughed. "Don't worry, Helen," she said. "There'll be a logical explanation for the face at the window."

The girls walked back to the front door of the mansion. Miss Flora and Aunt Rosemary stood there and immediately insisted upon knowing what had happened. As Helen told them, Nancy once more surveyed the outside of the window at which Helen had seen the terrifying face.

"I have a theory," she spoke up. "Our ghost simply leaned across from the end of the porch and held a mask in front of the window." Nancy stretched her arm out to demonstrate how this was possible.

"So that's why he didn't leave any footprints under the window," Helen said. "But he certainly got away from here fast." She suddenly laughed. "He must be on some ghosts' track team."

Her humor, Nancy was glad to see, relieved the tense situation. She had noticed Miss Flora leaning wearily on her daughter's arm.

"You'd better lie down and rest, Mother," Mrs. Hayes advised.

"I guess I will," Aunt Flora agreed.

It was suggested that the elderly woman use Aunt Rosemary's room, while the others continued the experiment with the chandelier.

Helen and Aunt Rosemary went into the parlor and waited as Nancy ascended the front stairway and went to Miss Flora's bedroom. Once more she began to rock from side to side. Downstairs, Aunt Rosemary and her niece were gazing intently at the ceiling.

"Look!" Helen exclaimed, pointing to the crystal chandelier. "It's moving!" In a moment it swung to the left, then back to the right.

"Nancy has proved that the ghost was up in my mother's room!" Aunt Rosemary said excitedly.

After a few minutes the rocking motion of the chandelier slackened and finally stopped. Nancy came hurrying down the steps.

"Did it work?" she called.

"Yes, it did," Aunt Rosemary replied. "Oh, Nancy, we must have two ghosts!"

"Why do you say that?" Helen asked.

"One rocking the chandelier, the other holding the horrible face up to the window. No one could have gone from Miss Flora's room to the front porch in such a short time. Oh, this complicates everything!"

"It certainly does," Nancy agreed. "The question is, are the two ghosts in cahoots? Or, it's just possible, there is only one. He could have disappeared from Miss Flora's room without our seeing him and somehow hurried to the first floor and let himself out the front door while we were upstairs. I'm convinced there is at least one secret entrance into this house, and maybe more. I think our next step should be to try to find it—or them."

"We'd better wash the luncheon dishes first," Aunt Rosemary suggested.

As she and the girls worked, they discussed the mystery, and Mrs. Hayes revealed that she had talked to her mother about leaving the house, whether or not she sold it.

"I thought we might at least go away for a little vacation, but Mother refuses to leave. She says she intends to remain right here until this ghost business is settled."

Helen smiled. "Nancy, my great-grandmother

is a wonderful woman. She has taught me a lot about courage and perseverance. I hope if I ever reach her age, I'll have half as much."

"Yes, she's an example to all of us," Aunt Rosemary concurred.

Nancy nodded. "I agree. I haven't known your mother long, Aunt Rosemary, but I think she is one of the dearest persons I've ever met."

"If Miss Flora won't leave," said Helen, "I guess that means we all stay."

"That's settled," said Nancy with a smile.

After the dishes were put away, the girls were ready to begin their search for a secret entrance into the mansion.

"Let's start with Miss Flora's room," Helen suggested.

"That's a logical place," Nancy replied, and took the lead up the stairway.

Every inch of the wall, which was paneled in maple halfway to the ceiling, was tapped. No hollow sound came from any section of it to indicate an open space behind. The bureau, dressing table, and bed were pulled away from the walls and Nancy carefully inspected every inch of the paneling for cracks or wide seams to indicate a concealed door.

"Nothing yet," she announced, and then decided to inspect the sides of the fireplace.

The paneled sides and brick front revealed nothing. Next, Nancy looked at the sides and rear of the stone interior. She could see nothing unusual, and the blackened stones did not look as if they had ever been disturbed.

She closed the damper which Helen had left open, and then suggested that the searchers transfer to another room on the second floor. But no trace of any secret entrance to the mansion could be found.

"I think we've had enough investigation for one day," Aunt Rosemary remarked.

Nancy was about to say that she was not tired and would like to continue. But she realized that Mrs. Hayes had made this suggestion because her mother was once more showing signs of fatigue and strain.

Helen, who also realized the situation, said, "Let's have an early supper. I'm starved!"

"I am, too," Nancy replied, laughing gaily.

The mood was contagious and soon Miss Flora seemed to have forgotten about her mansion being haunted. She sat in the kitchen while Aunt Rosemary and the girls cooked the meal.

"*Um,* steak and French fried potatoes, fresh peas, and yummy floating island for dessert," said Helen. "I can hardly wait."

"Fruit cup first," Aunt Rosemary announced, taking a bowl of fruit from the refrigerator.

Soon the group was seated at the table. Tactfully steering the conversation away from the mystery, Nancy asked Miss Flora to tell the group about parties and dances which had been held in the mansion long ago.

The elderly woman smiled in recollection. "I remember one story my husband told me of something that happened when he was a little boy," Miss Flora began. "His parents were holding a masquerade and he was supposed to be in bed fast asleep. His nurse had gone downstairs to talk to some of the servants. The music awakened my husband and he decided it would be great fun to join the guests.

" 'I'll put on a costume myself,' he said to himself. He knew there were some packed in a trunk in the attic." Miss Flora paused. "By the way, girls, I think that sometime while you are here you ought to see them. They're beautiful.

"Well, Everett went to the attic, opened the trunk, and searched until he found a soldier's outfit. It was very fancy—red coat and white trousers. He had quite a struggle getting it on and had to turn the coat sleeves way up. The knee britches came to his ankles, and the hat was so large it came down over his ears."

By this time Miss Flora's audience was laughing and Aunt Rosemary remarked, "My father really must have looked funny. Please go on, Mother."

"Little Everett came down the stairs and mingled with the masqueraders at the dance. For a while he wasn't noticed, then suddenly his mother discovered the queer-looking figure."

"And," Aunt Rosemary interrupted, "quickly put him back to bed, I'm sure."

Miss Flora laughed. "That's where you're wrong. The guests thought the whole thing was such fun that they insisted Everett stay. Some of the women danced with him—he went to dancing school and was an excellent dancer. Then they gave him some strawberries and cream and cake."

Helen remarked, "And then put him to bed."

Again Miss Flora laughed. "The poor little fellow never knew that he had fallen asleep while he was eating, and his father had to carry him upstairs. He was put into his little four-poster, costume and all. Of course his nurse was horrified, and I'm afraid that during the rest of the night the poor woman thought she would lose her position. But she didn't. In fact, she stayed with the family until all the children were grown up."

"Oh, that's a wonderful story!" said Nancy.

She was about to urge Miss Flora to tell another story when the telephone rang. Aunt Rosemary answered it, and then called to Nancy, "It's for you."

Nancy hurried to the hall, grabbed up the phone, and said, "Hello." A moment later she cried out, "Dad! How wonderful to hear from you!"

Mr. Drew said that he had not found Willie Wharton and certain clues seemed to indicate that he was not in Chicago, but in some other city.

"I have a few other matters to take care of that will keep me here until tomorrow night. How are you getting along?"

"I haven't solved the mystery yet," his daughter reported. "We've had some more strange happenings. I'll certainly be glad to see you here at Cliffwood. I know you can help me."

"All right, I'll come. But don't try to meet me. The time is too uncertain, and as a matter of fact, I may find that I'll have to stay here in Chicago."

Mr. Drew said he would come out to the mansion by taxi. Briefly Nancy related her experiences at Twin Elms, and after a little more conversation, hung up. When she rejoined the others at the table, she told them about Mr. Drew's promised visit.

"Oh, I'll be so happy to meet your father," said Miss Flora. "We may need legal advice in this mystery."

There was a pause after this remark, with everyone silent for a few moments. Suddenly each one in the group looked at the others, startled. From somewhere upstairs came the plaintive strains of violin music. Had the radio been turned on again by the ghost?

Nancy dashed from the table to find out.

CHAPTER VII

Frightening Eyes

WITHIN five seconds Nancy had reached the second floor. The violin playing suddenly ceased.

She raced into Miss Flora's room, from which the sounds had seemed to come. The radio was not on. Quickly Nancy felt the instrument to see if it were even slightly warm to prove it had been in use.

"The music wasn't being played on this," she told herself, finding the radio cool.

As Nancy dashed from the room, she almost ran into Helen. "What did you find out?" her friend asked breathlessly.

"Nothing so far," Nancy replied, as she raced into Aunt Rosemary's bedroom to check the bedside radio in there.

This instrument, too, felt cool to the touch.

She and Helen stood in the center of the room, puzzled frowns creasing their foreheads. "There *was* music, wasn't there?" Helen questioned.

"I distinctly heard it," Nancy replied. "But *where* is the person who played the violin? Or put a disk on a record player, or turned on a hidden radio? Helen, I'm positive an intruder comes into this mansion by some secret entrance and tries to frighten us all."

"And succeeds," Helen answered. "It's positively eerie."

"And dangerous," Nancy thought.

"Let's continue our search right after breakfast tomorrow," Helen proposed.

"We will," Nancy responded. "But in the meantime I believe Miss Flora and Aunt Rosemary, to say nothing of ourselves, need some police protection."

"I think you're right," Helen agreed. "Let's go downstairs and suggest it to the others."

The girls returned to the first floor and Nancy told Mrs. Hayes and her mother of the failure to find the cause of the violin playing, and what she had in mind.

"Oh dear, the police will only laugh at us," Miss Flora objected.

"Mother dear," said her daughter, "the captain and his men didn't believe us before because they thought we were imagining things. But Nancy and Helen heard music at two different times and they saw the chandelier rock. I'm sure that Captain Rossland will believe Nancy and send a guard out here."

Nancy smiled at Miss Flora. "I shan't ask the captain to believe in a ghost or even hunt for one. I think all we should request at the moment is that he have a man patrol the grounds here at night. I'm sure that we're perfectly safe while we're all awake, but I must admit I'd feel a little uneasy about going to bed wondering what that ghost may do next."

Mrs. Turnbull finally agreed to the plan and Nancy went to the telephone. Captain Rossland readily agreed to send a man out a little later.

"He'll return each night as long as you need him," the officer stated. "And I'll tell him not to ring the bell to tell you when he comes. If there is anyone who breaks into the mansion by a secret entrance, it would be much better if he does not know a guard is on duty."

"I understand," said Nancy.

When Miss Flora, her daughter, and the two girls went to bed, they were confident they would have a restful night. Nancy felt that if there was no disturbance, then it would indicate that the ghost's means of entry into Twin Elms was directly from the outside. "In which case," she thought, "it will mean he saw the guard and didn't dare come inside the house."

The young sleuth's desire for a good night's sleep was rudely thwarted as she awakened about midnight with a start. Nancy was sure she had heard a noise nearby. But now the house was quiet. Nancy listened intently, then finally got out of bed.

"Perhaps the noise I heard came from out-doors," she told herself.

Tiptoeing to a window, so that she would not awaken Helen, Nancy peered out at the moonlit grounds. Shadows made by tree branches, which swayed in a gentle breeze, moved back and forth across the lawn. The scent from a rose garden in full bloom was wafted to Nancy.

"What a heavenly night!" she thought.

Suddenly Nancy gave a start. A furtive figure had darted from behind a tree toward a clump of bushes. Was he the guard or the ghost? she wondered. As Nancy watched intently to see if she could detect any further movements of the mysteri-ous figure, she heard padding footsteps in the hall. In a moment there was a loud knock on her door.

"Nancy! Wake up! Nancy! Come quick!"

The voice was Miss Flora's, and she sounded ex-tremely frightened. Nancy sped across the room, unlocked her door, and opened it wide. By this time Helen was awake and out of bed.

"What happened?" she asked sleepily.

Aunt Rosemary had come into the hall also. Her mother did not say a word; just started back toward her own bedroom. The others followed, wondering what they would find. Moonlight brightened part of the room, but the area near the hall was dark.

"There! Up there!" Miss Flora pointed to a corner of the room near the hall.

Two burning eyes looked down on the watchers!

Instantly Nancy snapped on the wall light and the group gazed upward at a large brown owl perched on the old-fashioned, ornamental picture molding.

"Oh!" Aunt Rosemary cried out. "How did that bird ever get in here?"

The others did not answer at once. Then Nancy, not wishing to frighten Miss Flora, remarked as casually as she could, "It probably came down the chimney."

"But—" Helen started to say.

Nancy gave her friend a warning wink and Helen did not finish the sentence. Nancy was sure she was going to say that the damper had been closed and the bird could not possibly have flown into the room from the chimney. Turning to Miss Flora, Nancy asked whether or not her bedroom door had been locked.

"Oh, yes," the elderly woman insisted. "I wouldn't leave it unlocked for anything."

Nancy did not comment. Knowing that Miss Flora was a bit forgetful, she thought it quite possible that the door had not been locked. An intruder had entered, let the owl fly to the picture molding, then made just enough noise to awaken the sleeping woman.

To satisfy her own memory about the damper, Nancy went over to the fireplace and looked inside. The damper was closed.

"But if the door to the hall was locked," she reasoned, "then the ghost has some other way of getting into this room. And he escaped the detection of the guard."

"I don't want that owl in here all night," Miss Flora broke into Nancy's reverie. "We'll have to get it out."

"That's not going to be easy," Aunt Rosemary spoke up. "Owls have very sharp claws and beaks and they use them viciously on anybody who tries to disturb them. Mother, you come and sleep in my room the rest of the night. We'll chase the owl out in the morning."

Nancy urged Miss Flora to go with her daughter. "I'll stay here and try getting Mr. Owl out of the house. Have you a pair of old heavy gloves?"

"I have some in my room," Aunt Rosemary replied. "They're thick leather. I use them for gardening."

She brought them to Nancy, who put the gloves on at once. Then she suggested that Aunt Rosemary and her mother leave. Nancy smiled. "Helen and I will take over Operation Owl."

As the door closed behind the two women, Nancy dragged a chair to the corner of the room beneath the bird. She was counting on the fact that the bright overhead light had dulled the owl's vision and she would be able to grab it without too much trouble.

"Helen, will you open one of the screens, please?" she requested. "And wish me luck!"

"Don't let that thing get loose," Helen warned as she unfastened the screen and held it far out.

Nancy reached up and by stretching was just able to grasp the bird. In a lightning movement she had put her two hands around its body and imprisoned its claws. At once the owl began to bob its head and peck at her arms above the gloves. Wincing with pain, she stepped down from the chair and ran across the room.

The bird squirmed, darting its beak in first one direction, then another. But Nancy managed to hold the owl in such a position that most of the pecking missed its goal. She held the bird out the window, released it, and stepped back. Helen closed the screen and quickly fastened it.

"Oh!" Nancy said, gazing ruefully at her wrists which now showed several bloody digs from the owl's beak. "I'm glad that's over."

"And I am too," said Helen. "Let's lock Miss Flora's door from the outside, so that ghost can't bring in any owls to the rest of us."

Suddenly Helen grabbed Nancy's arm. "I just thought of something," she said. "There's supposed to be a police guard outside. Yet the ghost got in here without being seen."

"Either that, or there's a secret entrance to this

mansion which runs underground, probably to one of the outbuildings on the property."

Nancy now told about the furtive figure she had seen dart from behind a tree. "I must find out right away if he was the ghost or the guard. I'll do a little snooping around. It's possible the guard didn't show up." Nancy smiled. "But if he did, and he's any good, he'll find me!"

"All right," said Helen. "But, Nancy, do be careful. You're really taking awful chances to solve the mystery of Twin Elms."

Nancy laughed softly as she walked back to the girls' bedroom. She dressed quickly, then went downstairs, put the back-door key in her pocket, and let herself out of the house. Stealthily she went down the steps and glided to a spot back of some bushes.

Seeing no one around, she came from behind them and ran across the lawn to a large maple tree. She stood among the shadows for several moments, then darted out toward a building which in Colonial times had been used as the kitchen.

Halfway there, she heard a sound behind her and turned. A man stood in the shadows not ten feet away. Quick as a wink one hand flew to a holster on his hip.

"Halt!" he commanded.

CHAPTER VIII

A Startling Plunge

NANCY halted as directed and stood facing the man. "Who are you?" she asked.

"I'm a police guard, miss," the man replied. "Just call me Patrick. And who are you?"

Quickly Nancy explained and then asked to see his identification. He opened his coat, pulled out a leather case, and showed her his shield proving that he was a plain-clothes man. His name was Tom Patrick.

"Have you seen anyone prowling around the grounds?" Nancy asked him.

"Not a soul, miss. This place has been quieter than a cemetery tonight."

When the young sleuth told him about the furtive figure she had seen from the window, the detective laughed. "I believe you saw me," he said. "I guess I'm not so good at hiding as I thought I was."

Nancy laughed lightly. "Anyway, you soon nabbed me," she told him.

The two chatted for several minutes. Tom Patrick told Nancy that people in Cliffwood regarded Mrs. Turnbull as being a little queer. They said that if she thought her house was haunted, it was all in line with the stories of the odd people who had lived there from time to time during the past hundred years or so.

"Would this rumor make the property difficult to sell?" Nancy questioned the detective.

"It certainly would."

Nancy said she thought the whole thing was a shame. "Mrs. Turnbull is one of the loveliest women I've ever met and there's not a thing the matter with her, except that once in a while she is forgetful."

"You don't think that some of these happenings we've heard about are just pure imagination?" Tom Patrick asked.

"No, I don't."

Nancy now told him about the owl in Miss Flora's bedroom. "The door was locked, every screen was fastened, and the damper in the chimney closed. You tell me how the owl got in there."

Tom Patrick's eyes opened wide. "You say this happened only a little while ago?" he queried. When Nancy nodded, he added, "Of course I can't be everywhere on these grounds at once, but I've been round and round the building. I've never stopped walking since I arrived. I don't see how anyone could have gotten inside that mansion without my seeing him."

"I'll tell you my theory," said Nancy. "I believe there's a secret underground entrance from some other place on the grounds. It may be in one of these outbuildings. Anyway, tomorrow morning I'm going on a search for it."

"Well, I wish you luck," Tom Patrick said. "And if anything happens during the night, I'll let you know."

Nancy pointed to a window on the second floor. "That's my room," she said. "If you don't have a chance to use the door knocker, just throw a stone up against the screen to alert me. I'll wake up instantly, I know."

The guard promised to do this and Nancy went back into the mansion. She climbed the stairs and for a second time that night undressed. Helen had already gone back to sleep, so Nancy crawled into the big double bed noiselessly.

The two girls awoke the next morning about the same time and immediately Helen asked for full details of what Nancy had learned outdoors the night before. After hearing how her friend had been stopped by the guard, she shivered.

"You might have been in real danger, Nancy, not knowing who he was. You *must* be more careful. Suppose that man had been the ghost?"

Nancy laughed but made no reply. The girls

went downstairs and started to prepare breakfast. In a few minutes Aunt Rosemary and her mother joined them.

"Did you find out anything more last night?" Mrs. Hayes asked Nancy.

"Only that a police guard named Tom Patrick is on duty," Nancy answered.

As soon as breakfast was over, the young sleuth announced that she was about to investigate all the outbuildings on the estate.

"I'm going to search for an underground passage leading to the mansion. It's just possible that we hear no hollow sounds when we tap the walls, because of double doors or walls where the entrance is."

Aunt Rosemary looked at Nancy intently. "You are a real detective, Nancy. I see now why Helen wanted us to ask you to find our ghost."

Nancy's eyes twinkled. "I may have some instinct for sleuthing," she said, "but unless I can solve this mystery, it won't do any of us much good."

Turning to Helen, she suggested that they put on the old clothes they had brought with them.

Attired in sport shirts and jeans, the girls left the house. Nancy led the way first to the old icehouse. She rolled back the creaking, sliding door and gazed within. The tall, narrow building was about ten feet square. On one side were a series of sliding doors, one above the other.

"I've heard Miss Flora say," Helen spoke up, "that in days gone by huge blocks of ice were cut from the river when it was frozen over and dragged here on a sledge. The blocks were stored here and taken off from the top down through these various sliding doors."

"That story rather rules out the possibility of any underground passage leading from this building," said Nancy. "I presume there was ice in here most of the year."

The floor was covered with dank sawdust, and although Nancy was sure she would find nothing of interest beneath it, still she decided to take a look. Seeing an old, rusted shovel in one corner, she picked it up and began to dig. There was only dirt beneath the sawdust.

"Well, that clue fizzled out," Helen remarked, as she and Nancy started for the next building.

This had once been used as a smokehouse. It, too, had an earthen floor. In one corner was a small fireplace, where smoldering fires of hickory wood had once burned. The smoke had curled up a narrow chimney to the second floor, which was windowless.

"Rows and rows of huge chunks of pork hung up there on hooks to be smoked," Helen explained, "and days later turned into luscious hams and bacon."

There was no indication of a secret opening and Nancy went outside the small, two-story, peak-roofed structure and walked around. Up one side of the brick building and leading to a door above were the remnants of a ladder. Now only the sidepieces which had held the rungs remained.

"Give me a boost, will you, Helen?" Nancy requested. "I want to take a look inside."

Helen squatted on the ground and Nancy climbed to her shoulders. Then Helen, bracing her hands against the wall, straightened up. Nancy opened the half-rotted wooden door.

"No ghost here!" she announced.

Nancy jumped to the ground and started for the servants' quarters. But a thorough inspection of this brick-and-wood structure failed to reveal a clue to a secret passageway.

There was only one outbuilding left to investigate, which Helen said was the old carriage house. This was built of brick and was fairly large. No carriages stood on its wooden floor, but around the walls hung old harnesses and reins. Nancy paused a moment to examine one of the bridles. It was set with two hand-painted medallions of women's portraits.

Suddenly her reflection was interrupted by a scream. Turning, she was just in time to see Helen plunge through a hole in the floor. In a flash Nancy was across the carriage house and looking down into a gaping hole where the rotted floor had given way.

"Helen!" she cried out in alarm.

"I'm all right," came a voice from below. "Nice and soft down here. Please throw me your flash."

Nancy removed the flashlight from the pocket of her jeans and tossed it down.

"I thought maybe I'd discovered something," Helen said. "But this is just a plain old hole. Give me a hand, will you, so I can climb up?"

Nancy lay flat on the floor and with one arm grabbed a supporting beam that stood in the center of the carriage house. Reaching down with the other arm, she assisted Helen in her ascent.

"We'd better watch our step around here," Nancy said as her friend once more stood beside her.

"You're so right," Helen agreed, brushing dirt off her jeans. Helen's plunge had given Nancy an idea that there might be other openings in the floor and that one of them could be an entrance to a subterranean passage. But though she flashed her light over every inch of the carriage-house floor, she could discover nothing suspicious.

"Let's quit!" Helen suggested. "I'm a mess, and besides, I'm hungry."

"All right," Nancy agreed. "Are you game to search the cellar this afternoon?"

"Oh, sure."

After lunch they started to investigate the storerooms in the cellar. There was a cool stone room where barrels of apples had once been kept. There was another, formerly filled with bags of whole-wheat flour, barley, buckwheat, and oatmeal.

"And everything was grown on the estate," said Helen.

"Oh, it must have been perfectly wonderful," Nancy said. "I wish we could go back in time and see how life was in those days!"

"Maybe if we could, we'd know how to find that ghost," Helen remarked. Nancy thought so too.

As the girls went from room to room in the cellar, Nancy beamed her flashlight over every inch of wall and floor. At times, the young sleuth's pulse would quicken when she thought she had discovered a trap door or secret opening. But each time she had to admit failure—there was no evidence of either one in the cellar.

"This has been a discouraging day," Nancy remarked, sighing. "But I'm not giving up."

Helen felt sorry for her friend. To cheer Nancy, she said with a laugh, "Storeroom after storeroom but no room to store a ghost!"

Nancy had to laugh, and together the two girls ascended the stairway to the kitchen. After changing their clothes, they helped Aunt Rosemary prepare the evening dinner. When the group had eaten and later gathered in the parlor, Nancy reminded the others that she expected her father to arrive the next day.

"Dad didn't want me to bother meeting him,

but I just can't wait to see him. I think I'll meet all the trains from Chicago that stop here."

"I hope your father will stay with us for two or three days," Miss Flora spoke up. "Surely he'll have some ideas about our ghost."

"And good ones, too," Nancy said. "If he's on the early train, he'll have breakfast with us. I'll meet it at eight o'clock."

But later that evening Nancy's plans were suddenly changed. Hannah Gruen telephoned her to say that a man at the telegraph office had called the house a short time before to read a message from Mr. Drew. He had been unavoidably detained and would not arrive Wednesday.

"In the telegram your father said that he will let us know when he will arrive," the housekeeper added.

"I'm disappointed," Nancy remarked, "but I hope this delay means that Dad is. on the trail of Willie Wharton!"

"Speaking of Willie Wharton," said Hannah, "I heard something about him today."

"What was that?" Nancy asked.

"That he was seen down by the river right here in River Heights a couple of days ago!"

CHAPTER IX

A Worrisome Delay

"You say Willie Wharton was seen in River Heights down by the river?" Nancy asked unbelievingly.

"Yes," Hannah replied. "I learned it from our postman, Mr. Ritter, who is one of the people that sold property to the railroad. As you know, Nancy, Mr. Ritter is very honest and reliable. Well, he said he'd heard that some of the property owners were trying to horn in on this deal of Willie Wharton's for getting more money. But Mr. Ritter wouldn't have a thing to do with it—calls it a holdup."

"Did Mr. Ritter himself see Willie Wharton?" Nancy asked eagerly.

"No," the housekeeper replied. "One of the other property owners told him Willie was around."

"That man *could* be mistaken," Nancy suggested.

"Of course he might," Hannah agreed. "And I'm inclined to think he is. If your father is staying over in Chicago, it must be because of Willie Wharton."

Nancy did not tell Hannah what was racing through her mind. She said good night cheerfully, but actually she was very much worried.

"Maybe Willie Wharton *was* seen down by the river," she mused. "And maybe Dad was 'unavoidably detained' by an enemy of his in connection with the railroad bridge project. One of the dissatisfied property owners might have followed him to Chicago."

Or, she reflected further, it was not inconceivable that Mr. Drew had found Willie Wharton, only to have Willie hold the lawyer a prisoner.

As Nancy sat lost in anxious thought, Helen came into the hall. "Something the matter?" she asked.

"I don't know," Nancy replied, "but I have a feeling there is. Dad telegraphed to say that he wouldn't be here tomorrow. Instead of wiring, he always phones me or Hannah or his office when he is away and it seems strange that he didn't do so this time."

"You told me a few days ago that your father had been threatened," said Helen. "Are you afraid it has something to do with that?"

"Yes, I am."

"Is there anything I can do?" Helen offered.

"Thank you, Helen, but I think not. There isn't anything I can do either. We'll just have to wait and see what happens. Maybe I'll hear from Dad again."

Nancy looked so downcast that Helen searched her mind to find something which would cheer her friend. Suddenly Helen had an idea and went to speak to Miss Flora and Aunt Rosemary about it.

"I think it's a wonderful plan if Nancy will do it," Aunt Rosemary said.

Helen called Nancy from the hall and proposed that they all go to the attic to look in the big trunk containing the old costumes.

"We might even put them on," Miss Flora proposed, smiling girlishly.

"And you girls could dance the minuet," said Aunt Rosemary enthusiastically. "Mother plays the old spinet very well. Maybe she would play a minuet for you."

"I love your idea," said Nancy. She knew that the three were trying to boost her spirits and she appreciated it. Besides, what they had proposed sounded like fun.

All of them trooped up the creaky attic stairs. In their haste, none of the group had remembered to bring flashlights.

"I'll go downstairs and get a couple," Nancy offered.

"Never mind," Aunt Rosemary spoke up.

"There are some candles and holders right here. We keep them for emergencies."

She lighted two white candles which stood in old-fashioned, saucer-type brass holders and led the way to the costume trunk.

As Helen lifted the heavy lid, Nancy exclaimed in delight, "How beautiful the clothes are!"

She could see silks, satins, and laces at one side. At the other was a folded-up rose velvet robe. She and Helen lifted out the garments and held them up.

"They're really lovelier than our formal dance clothes today," Helen remarked. "Especially the men's!"

Miss Flora smiled. "And a lot more flattering!"

The entire trunk was unpacked, before the group selected what they would wear.

"This pale-green silk gown with the panniers would look lovely on you, Nancy," Miss Flora said. "And I'm sure it's just the right size, too."

Nancy surveyed the tiny waist of the ball gown. "I'll try it on," she said. Then laughingly she added, "But I'll probably have to hold my breath to close it in the middle. My, but the women in olden times certainly had slim waistlines!"

Helen was holding up a man's purple velvet suit. It had knee breeches and the waistcoat had a lace-ruffled front. There were a tricorn hat, long white stockings, and buckled slippers to complete the costume.

"I think I'll wear this and be your partner, Nancy," Helen said.

Taking off her pumps, she slid her feet into the buckled slippers. The others laughed aloud. A man with a foot twice the size of Helen's had once worn the slippers!

"Never mind. I'll stuff the empty space with paper," Helen announced gaily.

Miss Flora and Aunt Rosemary selected gowns for themselves, then opened a good-sized box at the bottom of the trunk. It contained various kinds of wigs worn in Colonial times. All were pure white and fluffy.

Carrying the costumes and wigs, the group descended to their bedrooms, where they changed into the fancy clothes, then went to the first floor. Miss Flora led the way into the room across the hall from the parlor. She said it once had been the drawing room. Later it had become a library, but the old spinet still stood in a corner.

Miss Flora sat down at the instrument and began to play Beethoven's "Minuet." Aunt Rosemary sat down beside her.

Nancy and Helen, dubbed by the latter, Master and Mistress Colonial America, began to dance. They clasped their right hands high in the air, then took two steps backward and made little bows. They circled, then strutted, and even put in a few steps with which no dancers in Colonial times would have been familiar.

Aunt Rosemary giggled and clapped. "I wish President Washington would come to see you," she said, acting out her part in the entertainment. "Mistress Nancy, prithee do an encore and Master Corning, wilt thou accompany thy fair lady?"

The girls could barely keep from giggling. Helen made a low bow to her aunt, her tricorn in her hand, and said, "At your service, my lady. Your every wish is my command!"

The minuet was repeated, then as Miss Flora stopped playing, the girls sat down.

"Oh, that was such fun!" said Nancy. "Some time I'd like to— Listen!" she commanded suddenly.

From outside the house they could hear loud shouting. "Come here! You in the house! Come here!"

Nancy and Helen dashed from their chairs to the front door. Nancy snapped on the porch light and the two girls raced outside.

"Over here!" a man's voice urged.

Nancy and Helen ran down the steps and out onto the lawn. Just ahead of them stood Tom Patrick, the police detective. In a viselike grip he was holding a thin, bent-over man whom the girls judged to be about fifty years of age.

"Is this your ghost?" the guard asked.

His prisoner was struggling to free himself but was unable to get loose. The girls hurried forward to look at the man.

"Is this your ghost?" the police guard asked

"I caught him sneaking along the edge of the grounds," Tom Patrick announced.

"Let me go!" the man cried out angrily. "I'm no ghost. What are you talking about?"

"You may not be a ghost," the detective said, "but you could be the thief who has been robbing this house."

"What!" his prisoner exclaimed. "I'm no thief! I live around here. Anyone will tell you I'm okay."

"What's your name and where do you live?" the detective prodded. He let the man stand up straight but held one of his arms firmly.

"My name's Albert Watson and I live over on Tuttle Road."

"What were you doing on this property?"

Albert Watson said he had been taking a short cut home. His wife had taken their car for the evening.

"I'd been to a friend's house. You can call him and verify what I'm saying. And you can call my wife, too. Maybe she's home now and she'll come and get me."

The guard reminded Albert Watson that he had not revealed why he was sneaking along the ground.

"Well," the prisoner said, "it was because of you. I heard downtown that there was a detective patrolling this place and I didn't want to bump into you. I was afraid of just what did happen."

The man relaxed a little. "I guess you're a pretty good guard at that."

Detective Patrick let go of Albert Watson's arm. "Your story sounds okay, but we'll go in the house and do some telephoning to find out if you're telling the truth."

"You'll find out all right. Why, I'm even a notary public! They don't give a notary's license to dishonest folks!" the trespasser insisted. Then he stared at Nancy and Helen, "What are you doing in those funny clothes?"

"We—are—we were having a little costume party," Helen responded. In the excitement she and Nancy had forgotten what they were wearing!

The two girls started for the house, with the men following. When Mr. Watson and the guard saw Miss Flora and Aunt Rosemary also in costume they gazed at the women in amusement.

Nancy introduced Mr. Watson. Miss Flora said she knew of him, although she had never met the man. Two phone calls by the guard confirmed Watson's story. In a little while his wife arrived at Twin Elms to drive her husband home, and Detective Patrick went back to his guard duty.

Aunt Rosemary then turned out all the lights on the first floor and she, Miss Flora, and the girls went upstairs. Bedroom doors were locked, and everyone hoped there would be no disturbance during the night.

"It was a good day, Nancy," said Helen, yawning, as she climbed into bed.

"Yes, it was," said Nancy. "Of course, I'm a little disappointed that we aren't farther along solving the mystery but maybe by this time tomorrow—" She looked toward Helen who did not answer. She was already sound asleep.

Nancy herself was under the covers a few minutes later. She lay staring at the ceiling, going over the various events of the past two days. As her mind recalled the scene in the attic when they were pulling costumes from the old trunk, she suddenly gave a start.

"That section of wall back of the trunk!" she told herself. "The paneling looked different somehow from the rest of the attic wall. Maybe it's movable and leads to a secret exit! Tomorrow I'll find out!"

CHAPTER X

The Midnight Watch

As soon as the two girls awoke the next morning, Nancy told Helen her plan.

"I'm with you," said Helen. "Oh, I do wish we could solve the mystery of the ghost! I'm afraid that it's beginning to affect Miss Flora's health and yet she won't leave Twin Elms."

"Maybe we can get Aunt Rosemary to keep her in the garden most of the day," Nancy suggested. "It's perfectly beautiful outside. We might even serve lunch under the trees."

"I'm sure they'd love that," said Helen. "As soon as we get downstairs, let's propose it."

Both women liked the suggestion. Aunt Rosemary had guessed their strategy and was appreciative of it.

"I'll wash and dry the dishes," Nancy offered when breakfast was over. "Miss Flora, why don't you and Aunt Rosemary go outside right now and take advantage of this lovely sunshine?"

The frail, elderly woman smiled. There were deep circles under her eyes, indicating that she had had a sleepless night.

"And I'll run the vacuum cleaner around and dust this first floor in less than half an hour," Helen said merrily.

Her relatives caught the spirit of her enthusiasm and Miss Flora remarked, "I wish you girls lived here all the time. Despite our troubles, you have brought a feeling of gaiety back into our lives."

Both girls smiled at the compliment. As soon as the two women had gone outdoors, the girls set to work with a will. At the end of the allotted half hour, the first floor of the mansion was spotless. Nancy and Helen next went to the second floor, quickly made the beds, and tidied the bathrooms.

"And now for that ghost!" said Helen, brandishing her flashlight.

Nancy took her own from a bureau drawer.

"Let's see if we can figure out how to climb these attic stairs without making them creak," Nancy suggested. "Knowing how may come in handy some time."

This presented a real challenge. Every inch of each step was tried before the girls finally worked out a pattern to follow in ascending the stairway noiselessly.

Helen laughed. "This will certainly be a

memory test, Nancy. I'll rehearse our directions. First step, put your foot to the left near the wall. Second step, right center. Third step, against the right wall. I'll need three feet to do that!"

Nancy laughed too. "For myself, I think I'll skip the second step. Let's see. On the fourth and fifth it's all right to step in the center, but on the sixth you hug the left wall, on the seventh, the right wall—"

Helen interrupted. "But if you step on the eighth any place, it will creak. So you skip it."

"Nine, ten, and eleven are okay," Nancy recalled. "But from there to fifteen at the top we're in trouble."

"Let's see if I remember," said Helen. "On twelve, you go left, then right, then right again. How can you do that without a jump and losing your balance and tumbling down?"

"How about skipping fourteen and then stretching as far as you can to reach the top one at the left where it doesn't squeak," Nancy replied. "Let's go!"

She and Helen went back to the second floor and began what was meant to be a silent ascent. But both of them made so many mistakes at first the creaking was terrific. Finally, however, the girls had the silent spots memorized perfectly and went up noiselessly.

Nancy clicked on her flashlight and swung it onto the nearest wood-paneled wall. Helen stared at it, then remarked, "This isn't made of long panels from ceiling to floor. It's built of small pieces."

"That's right," said Nancy. "But see if you don't agree with me that the spot back of the costume trunk near the chimney looks a little different. The grain doesn't match the other wood."

The girls crossed the attic and Nancy beamed her flashlight over the suspected paneling.

"It does look different," Helen said. "This could be a door, I suppose. But there's no knob or other hardware on it." She ran her finger over a section just above the floor, following the cracks at the edge of a four-by-two-and-a-half-foot space.

"If it's a secret door," said Nancy, "the knob is on the other side."

"How are we going to open it?" Helen questioned.

"We might try prying the door open," Nancy proposed. "But first I want to test it."

She tapped the entire panel with her knuckles. A look of disappointment came over her face. "There's certainly no hollow space behind it," she said.

"Let's make sure," said Helen. "Suppose I go downstairs and get a screw driver and hammer? We'll see what happens when we drive the screw driver through this crack."

"Good idea, Helen."

While she was gone, Nancy inspected the rest

of the attic walls and floor. She did not find another spot which seemed suspicious. By this time Helen had returned with the tools. Inserting the screw driver into one of the cracks, she began to pound on the handle of it with the hammer.

Nancy watched hopefully. The screw driver went through the crack very easily but immediately met an obstruction on the other side. Helen pulled the screw driver out. "Nancy, you try your luck."

The young sleuth picked a different spot, but the results were the same. There was no open space behind that portion of the attic wall.

"My hunch wasn't so good," said Nancy.

Helen suggested that they give up and go downstairs. "Anyway, I think the postman will be here soon." She smiled. "I'm expecting a letter from Jim. Mother said she would forward all my mail."

Nancy did not want to give up the search yet. But she nodded in agreement and waved her friend toward the stairs. Then the young detective sat down on the floor and cupped her chin in her hands. As she stared ahead, Nancy noticed that Helen, in her eagerness to meet the postman, had not bothered to go quietly down the attic steps. It sounded as if Helen had picked the squeakiest spot on each step!

Nancy heard Helen go out the front door and suddenly realized that she was in the big mansion all alone. "That may bring the ghost on a visit," she thought. "If he is around, he may think I went outside with Helen! And I may learn where the secret opening is!"

Nancy sat perfectly still, listening intently. Suddenly she flung her head up. Was it her imagination, or did she hear the creak of steps? She was not mistaken. Nancy strained her ears, trying to determine from where the sounds were coming.

"I'm sure they're not from the attic stairs or the main staircase. And not the back stairway. Even if the ghost was in the kitchen and unlocked the door to the second floor, he'd know that the one at the top of the stairs was locked from the other side."

Nancy's heart suddenly gave a leap. She was positive that the creaking sounds were coming from somewhere behind the attic wall!

"A secret staircase!" she thought excitedly. "Maybe the ghost is entering the second floor!"

Nancy waited until the sounds stopped, then she got to her feet, tiptoed noiselessly down the attic steps and looked around. She could hear nothing. Was the ghost standing quietly in one of the bedrooms? Probably Miss Flora's?

Treading so lightly that she did not make a sound, Nancy peered into each room as she reached it. But no one was in any of them.

"Maybe he's on the first floor!" Nancy thought. She descended the main stairway, hugging the wall so she would not make a sound. Reaching the first floor, Nancy peered into the parlor. No one was there. She looked in the library, the dining room, and the kitchen. She saw no one.

"Well, the ghost didn't come into the house after all," Nancy concluded. "He may have intended to, but changed his mind."

She felt more certain than at any time, however, that there was a secret entrance to Twin Elms Mansion from a hidden stairway. But how to find it? Suddenly the young sleuth snapped her fingers. "I know what I'll do! I'll set a trap for that ghost!"

She reflected that he had taken jewelry, but those thefts had stopped. Apparently he was afraid to go to the second floor.

"I wonder if anything is missing from the first floor," she mused. "Maybe he has taken silverware or helped himself to some food."

Going to the back door, Nancy opened it and called to Helen, who was now seated in the garden with Miss Flora and Aunt Rosemary. "What say we start lunch?" she called, not wishing to distress Miss Flora by bringing up the subject of the mystery.

"Okay," said Helen. In a few moments she joined Nancy, who asked if her friend had received a letter.

Helen's eyes sparkled. "I sure did. Oh, Nancy, I can hardly wait for Jim to get home!"

Nancy smiled. "The way you describe him, I can hardly wait to see him myself." Then she told Helen the real reason she had called her into the kitchen. She described the footsteps on what she was sure was a hidden, creaking stairway, then added, "If we discover that food or something else is missing we'll know he's been here again."

Helen offered to inspect the flat silver. "I know approximately how many pieces should be in the buffet drawer," she said.

"And I'll look over the food supplies," Nancy suggested. "I have a pretty good idea what was in the refrigerator and on the pantry shelf."

It was not many minutes before each of the girls discovered articles missing. Helen said that nearly a dozen teaspoons were gone and Nancy figured that several cans of food, some eggs, and a quart of milk had been taken.

"It just seems impossible to catch that thief," Helen said with a sigh.

On a sudden hunch Nancy took down from the wall a memo pad and pencil which hung there. Putting a finger to her lips to indicate that Helen was not to comment, Nancy wrote on the sheet:

"I think the only way to catch the ghost is to trap him. I believe he has one or more microphones hidden some place and that he hears all our plans."

Nancy looked up at Helen, who nodded silently. Nancy continued to write, "I don't want to worry

Miss Flora or Aunt Rosemary, so let's keep our plans a secret. I suggest that we go to bed tonight as usual and carry on a conversation about our plans for tomorrow. But actually we won't take off our clothes. Then about midnight let's tiptoe downstairs to watch. I'll wait in the kitchen. Do you want to stay in the living room?"

Again Helen nodded. Nancy, thinking that they had been quiet too long, and that if there was an eavesdropper nearby he might become suspicious, said aloud, "What would Miss Flora and Aunt Rosemary like for lunch, Helen?"

"Why, uh—" Helen found it hard to transfer to the new subject. "They—uh—both love soup."

"Then I'll make cream of chicken soup," said Nancy. "Hand me a can of chicken and rice, will you? And I'll get the milk."

As Helen was doing this, Nancy lighted a match, held her recently written note over the sink, and set fire to the paper.

Helen smiled. "Nancy thinks of everything," she said to herself.

The girls chatted gaily as they prepared the food and finally carried four trays out to the garden. They did not mention their midnight plan. The day in the garden was proving to be most beneficial to Miss Flora, and the girls were sure she would sleep well that night.

Nancy's plan was followed to the letter. Just

as the grandfather clock in the hall was striking midnight, Nancy arrived in the kitchen and sat down to await developments. Helen was posted in a living-room chair near the hall doorway. Moonlight streamed into both rooms but the girls had taken seats in the shadows.

Helen was mentally rehearsing the further instructions which Nancy had written to her during the afternoon. The young sleuth had suggested that if Helen should see anyone, she was to run to the front door, open it, and yell "Police!" At the same time she was to try to watch where the intruder disappeared.

The minutes ticked by. There was not a sound in the house. Then suddenly Nancy heard the front door open with a bang and Helen's voice yell loudly and clearly:

"Police! Help! Police!"

CHAPTER XI

An Elusive Ghost

By the time Nancy reached the front hall, Tom Patrick, the police guard, had rushed into the house. "Here I am!" he called. "What's the matter?"

Helen led the way into the living room, and switched on the chandelier light.

"That sofa next to the fireplace!" she said in a trembling voice. "It moved! I saw it move!"

"You mean somebody moved it?" the detective asked.

"I—I don't know," Helen replied. "I couldn't see anybody."

Nancy walked over to the old-fashioned sofa, set in the niche alongside the fireplace. Certainly the piece was in place now. If the ghost had moved it, he had returned the sofa to its original position.

"Let's pull it out and see what we can find," Nancy suggested.

She tugged at one end, while the guard pulled the other. It occurred to Nancy that a person who moved it alone would have to be very strong.

"Do you think your ghost came up through a trap door or something?" the detective asked.

Neither of the girls replied. They had previously searched the area, and even now as they looked over every inch of the floor and the three walls surrounding the high sides of the couch, they could detect nothing that looked like an opening.

By this time Helen looked sheepish. "I—I guess I was wrong," she said finally. Turning to the police guard, she said, "I'm sorry to have taken you away from your work."

"Don't feel too badly about it. But I'd better get back to my guard duty," the man said, and left the house.

"Oh, Nancy!" Helen cried out. "I'm so sorry!"

She was about to say more but Nancy put a finger to her lips. They could use the same strategy for trapping the thief at another time. In case the thief might be listening, Nancy did not want to give away their secret.

Nancy felt that after all the uproar the ghost would not appear again that night. She motioned to Helen that they would go quietly upstairs and get some sleep. Hugging the walls of the stairway once more, they ascended noiselessly, tiptoed to their room, and got into bed.

"I'm certainly glad I didn't wake up Miss Flora and Aunt Rosemary," said Helen sleepily as she whispered good night.

Though Nancy had been sure the ghost would not enter the mansion again that night, she discovered in the morning that she had been mistaken. More food had been stolen sometime between midnight and eight o'clock when she and Helen started breakfast. Had the ghost taken it for personal use or only to worry the occupants of Twin Elms?

"I missed my chance this time," Nancy murmured to her friend. "After this, I'd better not trust what that ghost's next move may be!"

At nine o'clock Hannah Gruen telephoned the house. Nancy happened to answer the ring and after the usual greetings was amazed to hear Hannah say, "I'd like to speak to your father."

"Why, Dad isn't here!" Nancy told her. "Don't you remember—the telegram said he wasn't coming?"

"He's not there!" Hannah exclaimed. "Oh, this is bad, Nancy—very bad."

"What do you mean, Hannah?" Nancy asked fearfully.

The housekeeper explained that soon after receiving the telegram on Tuesday evening, Mr. Drew himself had phoned. "He wanted to know if you were still in Cliffwood, Nancy. When I told him yes, he said he would stop off there on his way home Wednesday."

Nancy was frightened, but she asked steadily, "Hannah, did you happen to mention the telegram to him?"

"No, I didn't," the housekeeper replied. "I didn't think it was necessary."

"Hannah darling," said Nancy, almost on the verge of tears, "I'm afraid that telegram was a hoax!"

"A hoax!" Mrs. Gruen cried out.

"Yes. Dad's enemies sent it to keep me from meeting him!"

"Oh, Nancy," Hannah wailed, "you don't suppose those enemies that Mr. Gomber warned you about have waylaid your father and are keeping him prisoner?"

"I'm afraid so," said Nancy. Her knees began to quake and she sank into the chair alongside the telephone table.

"What'll we do?" Hannah asked. "Do you want me to notify the police?"

"Not yet. Let me do a little checking first."

"All right, Nancy. But let me know what happens."

"I will."

Nancy put the phone down, then looked at the various telephone directories which lay on the table. Finding one which contained River

Heights numbers, she looked for the number of the telegraph office and put in a call. She asked the clerk who answered to verify that there had been a telegram from Mr. Drew on Tuesday.

After a few minutes wait, the reply came. "We have no record of such a telegram."

Nancy thanked the clerk and hung up. By this time her hands were shaking with fright. What had happened to her father?

Getting control of herself, Nancy telephoned in turn to the airport, the railroad station, and the bus lines which served Cliffwood. She inquired about any accidents which might have occurred on trips from Chicago the previous day or on Tuesday night. In each case she was told there had been none.

"Oh, what shall I do?" Nancy thought in dismay.

Immediately an idea came to her and she put in a call to the Chicago hotel where her father had registered. Although she thought it unlikely, it was just possible that he had changed his mind again and was still there. But a conversation with the desk clerk dashed this hope.

"No, Mr. Drew is not here. He checked out Tuesday evening. I don't know his plans, but I'll connect you with the head porter. He may be able to help you."

In a few seconds Nancy was asking the porter what he could tell her to help clear up the mystery of her father's disappearance. "All I know, miss, is that your father told me he was taking a sleeper train and getting off somewhere Wednesday morning to meet his daughter."

"Thank you. Oh, thank you very much," said Nancy. "You've helped me a great deal."

So her father had taken the train home and probably had reached the Cliffwood station! Next she must find out what had happened to him after that!

Nancy told Aunt Rosemary and Helen what she had learned, then got in her convertible and drove directly to the Cliffwood station. There she spoke to the ticket agent. Unfortunately, he could not identify Mr. Drew from Nancy's description as having been among the passengers who got off either of the two trains arriving from Chicago on Wednesday.

Nancy went to speak to the taximen. Judging by the line of cabs, she decided that all the drivers who served the station were on hand at the moment. There had been no outgoing trains for nearly an hour and an incoming express was due in about fifteen minutes.

"I'm in luck," the young detective told herself. "Surely one of these men must have driven Dad."

She went from one to another, but each of them denied having carried a passenger of Mr. Drew's description the day before.

By this time Nancy was in a panic. She hurried inside the station to a telephone booth and called the local police station. Nancy asked to speak to the captain and in a moment he came on the line.

"Captain Rossland speaking," he said crisply.

Nancy poured out her story. She told of the warning her father had received in River Heights and her fear that some enemy of his was now detaining the lawyer against his will.

"This is very serious, Miss Drew," Captain Rossland stated. "I will put men on the case at once," he said.

As Nancy left the phone booth, a large, gray-haired woman walked up to her. "Pardon me, miss, but I couldn't help overhearing what you said. I believe maybe I can help you."

Nancy was surprised and slightly suspicious. Maybe this woman was connected with the abductors and planned to make Nancy a prisoner too by promising to take her to her father!

"Don't look so frightened," the woman said, smiling. "All I wanted to tell you is that I'm down here at the station every day to take a train to the next town. I'm a nurse and I'm on a case over there right now."

"I see," Nancy said.

"Well, yesterday I was here when the Chicago train came in. I noticed a tall, handsome man— such as you describe your father to be—step off the train. He got into the taxi driven by a man named Harry. I have a feeling that for some reason the cabbie isn't telling the truth. Let's talk to him."

Nancy followed the woman, her heart beating furiously. She was ready to grab at any straw to get a clue to her father's whereabouts!

"Hello, Miss Skade," the taximan said. "How are you today?"

"Oh, I'm all right," the nurse responded. "Listen, Harry. You told this young lady that you didn't carry any passenger yesterday that looked like her father. Now I saw one get into your cab. What about it?"

Harry hung his head. "Listen, miss," he said to Nancy, "I got three kids and I don't want nothin' to happen to 'em. See?"

"What do you mean?" Nancy asked, puzzled.

When the man did not reply, Miss Skade said, "Now look, Harry. This girl's afraid that her father has been kidnaped. It's up to you to tell her all you know."

"Kidnaped!" the taximan shouted. "Oh, goodnight! Now I don't know what to do."

Nancy had a sudden thought. "Has somebody been threatening you, Harry?" she asked.

The cab driver's eyes nearly popped from his head. "Well," he said, "since you've guessed it, I'd better tell you everything I know."

He went on to say that he had taken a passenger who fitted Mr. Drew's description toward Twin

Elms where he had said he wanted to go. "Just as we were leaving the station, two other men came up and jumped into my cab. They said they were going a little farther than that and would I take them? Well, about halfway to Twin Elms, one of those men ordered me to pull up to the side of the road and stop. He told me the stranger had blacked out. He and his buddy jumped out of the car and laid the man on the grass."

"How ill was he?" Nancy asked.

"I don't know. He was unconscious. Just then another car came along behind us and stopped. The driver got out and offered to take your father to a hospital. The two men said okay."

Nancy took heart. Maybe her father was in a hospital and had not been abducted at all! But a moment later her hopes were again dashed when Harry said:

"I told those guys I'd be glad to drive the sick man to a hospital, but one of them turned on me, shook his fist, and yelled, 'You just forget everything that's happened or it'll be too bad for you and your kids!'"

"Oh!" Nancy cried out, and for a second everything seemed to swim before her eyes. She clutched the door handle of the taxi for support.

There was no question now but that her father had been drugged, then kidnaped!

CHAPTER XII

The Newspaper Clue

Miss Skade grabbed Nancy. "Do you feel ill?" the nurse asked quickly.

"Oh, I'll be all right," Nancy replied. "This news has been a great shock to me."

"Is there any way I can help you?" the woman questioned. "I'd be very happy to."

"Thank you, but I guess not," the young sleuth said. Smiling ruefully, she added, "But I must get busy and do something about this."

The nurse suggested that perhaps Mr. Drew was in one of the local hospitals. She gave Nancy the names of the three in town.

"I'll get in touch with them at once," the young detective said. "You've been most kind. And here comes your train, Miss Skade. Good-by and again thanks a million for your help!"

Harry climbed out of his taxi and went to stand at the platform to signal passengers for his cab. Nancy hurried after him, and before the train

came in, asked if he would please give her a description of the two men who had been with her
father.

"Well, both of them were dark and kind of athletic-looking. Not what I'd call handsome. One
of 'em had an upper tooth missing. And the other
fellow—his left ear was kind of crinkled, if you
know what I mean."

"I understand," said Nancy. "I'll give a description of the two men to the police."

She went back to the telephone booth and
called each of the three hospitals, asking if anyone by the name of Carson Drew had been admitted or possibly a patient who was not conscious
and had no identification. Only Mercy Hospital
had a patient who had been unconscious since the
day before. He definitely was not Mr. Drew—
he was Chinese!

Sure now that her father was being held in some
secret hiding place, Nancy went at once to police
headquarters and related the taximan's story.

Captain Rossland looked extremely concerned.
"This is alarming, Miss Drew," he said, "but I feel
sure we can trace that fellow with the crinkly ear
and we'll make him tell us where your father is!
I doubt, though, that there is anything you can do.
You'd better leave it to the police."

Nancy said nothing. She was reluctant to give
up even trying to do something, but she acqui
esced.

"In the meantime," said the officer, "I'd advise you to remain at Twin Elms and concentrate on solving the mystery there. From what you tell me about your father, I'm sure he'll be able to get out of the difficulty himself, even before the police find him."

Aloud, Nancy promised to stay on call in case Captain Rossland might need her. But in her own mind the young sleuth determined that if she got any kind of a lead concerning her father, she was most certainly going to follow it up.

Nancy left police headquarters and strolled up the street, deep in thought. "Instead of things getting better, all my problems seem to be getting worse. Maybe I'd better call Hannah."

Since she had been a little girl, Nancy had found solace in talking to Hannah Gruen. The housekeeper had always been able to give her such good advice!

Nancy went into a drugstore and entered one of the telephone booths. She called the Drew home in River Heights and was pleased when Mrs. Gruen answered. The housekeeper was aghast to learn Nancy's news but said she thought Captain Rossland's advice was sound.

"You've given the police the best leads in the world and I believe that's all you can do. But wait—" the housekeeper suddenly said. "If I were you, Nancy, I'd call up those railroad lawyers and tell them exactly what has happened. Your father's disappearance is directly concerned with that bridge project, I'm sure, and the lawyers may have some ideas about where to find him."

"That's a wonderful suggestion, Hannah," said Nancy. "I'll call them right away."

But when the young detective phoned the railroad lawyers, she was disappointed to learn that all the men were out to lunch and none of them would return before two o'clock.

"Oh dear!" Nancy sighed. "Well, I guess I'd better get a snack while waiting for them to come back." But in her worried state she did not feel like eating.

There was a food counter at the rear of the drugstore and Nancy made her way to it. Perching on a high-backed stool, she read the menu over and over. Nothing appealed to her. When the counterman asked her what she wanted, Nancy said frankly she did not know—she was not very hungry.

"Then I recommend our split-pea soup," he told her. "It's homemade and out of this world."

Nancy smiled at him. "I'll take your advice and try it."

The hot soup was delicious. By the time she had finished it, Nancy's spirits had risen considerably.

"And how about some custard pie?" the counterman inquired. "It's just like Mother used to make."

"All right," Nancy answered, smiling at the solicitous young man. The pie was ice cold and proved to be delicious. When Nancy finished eating it, she glanced at her wrist watch. It was only one-thirty. Seeing a rack of magazines, she decided to while away the time reading in her car.

She purchased a magazine of detective stories, one of which proved to be so intriguing that the half hour went by quickly. Promptly at two o'clock Nancy returned to the phone booth and called the offices of the railroad lawyers. The switchboard operator connected her with Mr. Anthony Barradale and Nancy judged from his voice that he was fairly young. Quickly she told her story.

"Mr. Drew being held a prisoner!" Mr. Barradale cried out. "Well, those underhanded property owners are certainly going to great lengths to gain a few dollars."

"The police are working on the case, but I thought perhaps your firm would like to take a hand also," Nancy told the lawyer.

"We certainly will," the young man replied. "I'll speak to our senior partner about it. I know he will want to start work at once on the case."

"Thank you," said Nancy. She gave the address and telephone number of Twin Elms and asked that the lawyers get in touch with her there if any news should break.

"We'll do that," Mr. Barradale promised.

Nancy left the drugstore and walked back to her car. Climbing in, she wondered what her next move ought to be.

"One thing is sure," she thought. "Work is the best antidote for worry. I'll get back to Twin Elms and do some more sleuthing there."

As she drove along, Nancy reflected about the ghost entering Twin Elms mansion by a subterranean passage. Since she had found no sign of one in any of the outbuildings on the estate, it occurred to her that possibly it led from an obscure cave, either natural or man-made. Such a device would be a clever artifice for an architect to use.

Taking a little-used road that ran along one side of the estate, Nancy recalled having seen a long, grassed-over hillock which she had assumed to be an old aqueduct. Perhaps this was actually the hidden entrance to Twin Elms!

She parked her car at the side of the road and took a flashlight from the glove compartment. In anticipation of finding the answer to the riddle, Nancy crossed the field, and as she came closer to the beginning of the huge mound, she could see stones piled up. Getting nearer, she realized that it was indeed the entrance to a rocky cave.

"Well, maybe this time I've found it!" she thought, hurrying forward.

The wind was blowing strongly and tossed her hair about her face. Suddenly a freakish gust swept a newspaper from among the rocks and scattered the pages helter-skelter.

Nancy was more excited than ever. The newspaper meant a human being had been there not too long ago! The front page sailed toward her. As she grabbed it up, she saw to her complete astonishment that the paper was a copy of the *River Heights Gazette.* The date was the Tuesday before.

"Someone interested in River Heights has been here very recently!" the young sleuth said to herself excitedly.

Who was the person? Her father? Gomber? Who?

Wondering if the paper might contain any clue, Nancy dashed around to pick up all the sheets. As she spread them out on the ground, she noticed a hole in the page where classified ads appeared.

"This may be a very good clue!" Nancy thought. "As soon as I get back to the house, I'll call Hannah and have her look up Tuesday's paper to see what was in that ad."

It suddenly occurred to Nancy that the person who had brought the paper to the cave might be inside at this very moment. She must watch her step; he might prove to be an enemy!

"This may be where Dad is being held a prisoner!" Nancy thought wildly.

Flashlight in hand, and her eyes darting intently

about, Nancy proceeded cautiously into the cave. Five feet, ten. She saw no one. Fifteen more. Twenty. Then Nancy met a dead end. The empty cave was almost completely round and had no other opening.

"Oh dear, another failure," Nancy told herself disappointedly, as she retraced her steps. "My only hope now is to learn something important from the ad in the paper."

Nancy walked back across the field. Her eyes were down, as she automatically looked for footprints. But presently she looked up and stared in disbelief.

A man was standing alongside her car, examining it. His back was half turned toward Nancy, so she could not see his face very well. But he had an athletic build and his left ear was definitely crinkly!

CHAPTER XIII

The Crash

THE STRANGER inspecting Nancy's car must have heard her coming. Without turning around, he dodged back of the automobile and started off across the field in the opposite direction.

"He certainly acts suspiciously. He must be the man with the crinkly ear who helped abduct my father!" Nancy thought excitedly.

Quickly she crossed the road and ran after him as fast as she could, hoping to overtake him. But the man had had a good head start. Also, his stride was longer than Nancy's and he could cover more ground in the same amount of time.

The far corner of the irregular-shaped field ended at the road on which Riverview Manor stood. When Nancy reached the highway, she was just in time to see the stranger leap into a parked car and drive off.

The young detective was exasperated. She had

had only a glimpse of the man's profile. If only she could have seen him full face or caught the license number of his car!

"I wonder if he's the one who dropped the newspaper?" she asked herself. "Maybe he's from River Heights!" She surmised that the man himself was not one of the property owners but he might have been hired by Willie Wharton or one of the owners to help abduct Mr. Drew.

"I'd better hurry to a phone and report this," Nancy thought.

She ran all the way back across the field, stepped into her own car, turned it around, and headed for Twin Elms. When Nancy arrived, she sped to the telephone in the hall and dialed Cliffwood Police Headquarters. In a moment she was talking to the captain and gave him her latest information.

"It certainly looks as if you picked up a good clue, Miss Drew," the officer remarked. "I'll send out an alarm immediately to have this man picked up."

"I suppose there is no news of my father," Nancy said.

"I'm afraid not. But a couple of our men talked to the taxi driver Harry and he gave us a pretty good description of the man who came along the road while your father was lying unconscious on the grass—the one who offered to take him to the hospital."

"What did he look like?" Nancy asked.

The officer described the man as being in his early fifties, short, and rather heavy-set. He had shifty pale-blue eyes.

"Well," Nancy replied, "I can think of several men who would fit that description. Did he have any outstanding characteristics?"

"Harry didn't notice anything, except that the fellow's hands didn't look as if he did any kind of physical work. The taximan said they were kind of soft and pudgy."

"Well, that eliminates all the men I know who are short, heavy-set and have pale-blue eyes. None of them has hands like that."

"It'll be a good identifying feature," the police officer remarked. "Well, I guess I'd better get that alarm out."

Nancy said good-by and put down the phone. She waited several seconds for the line to clear, then picked up the instrument again and called Hannah Gruen. Before Nancy lay the sheet of newspaper from which the advertisement had been torn.

"The Drew residence," said a voice on the phone.

"Hello, Hannah. This is Nancy."

"How are you, dear? Any news?" Mrs. Gruen asked quickly.

"I haven't found Dad yet," the young detective replied. "And the police haven't either. But I've picked up a couple of clues."

"Tell me about them," the housekeeper requested excitedly.

Nancy told her about the man with the crinkly ear and said she was sure that the police would soon capture him. "If he'll only talk, we may find out where Dad is being held."

"Oh, I hope so!" Hannah sighed. "Don't get discouraged, Nancy."

At this point Helen came into the hall, and as she passed Nancy on her way to the stairs, smiled at her friend. The young sleuth was about to ask Hannah to get the Drews' Tuesday copy of the *River Heights Gazette* when she heard a cracking noise overhead. Immediately she decided the ghost might be at work again.

"Hannah, I'll call you back later," Nancy said and put down the phone.

She had no sooner done this than Helen screamed, "Nancy, run! The ceiling!" She herself started for the front door.

Nancy, looking up, saw a tremendous crack in the ceiling just above the girls' heads. The next instant the whole ceiling crashed down on them! They were thrown to the floor.

"Oh!" Helen moaned. She was covered with lath and plaster, and had been hit hard on the head. But she managed to call out from under the debris, "Nancy, are you all right?" There was no answer.

The whole ceiling crashed down on them!

The tremendous noise had brought Miss Flora and Aunt Rosemary on a run from the kitchen. They stared in horror at the scene before them. Nancy lay unconscious and Helen seemed too dazed to move.

"Oh my! Oh my!" Miss Flora exclaimed.

She and Aunt Rosemary began stepping over the lath and plaster, which by now had filled the air with dust. They sneezed again and again but made their way forward nevertheless.

Miss Flora, reaching Helen's side, started pulling aside chunks of broken plaster and lath. Finally, she helped her great-granddaughter to her feet.

"Oh, my dear, you're hurt!" she said solicitously.

"I'll—be—all right—in a minute," Helen insisted, choking with the dust. "But Nancy—"

Aunt Rosemary had already reached the unconscious girl. With lightning speed, she threw aside the debris which almost covered Nancy. Whipping a handkerchief from her pocket, she gently laid it over Nancy's face, so that she would not breathe in any more of the dust.

"Helen, do you feel strong enough to help me carry Nancy into the library?" she asked. "I'd like to lay her on the couch there."

"Oh, yes, Aunt Rosemary. Do you think Nancy is badly hurt?" she asked worriedly.

"I hope not."

At this moment Nancy stirred. Then her arm

moved upward and she pulled the handkerchief from her face. She blinked several times as if unable to recall where she was.

"You'll be all right, Nancy," said Aunt Rosemary kindly. "But I don't want you to breathe this dust. Please keep the handkerchief over your nose." She took it from Nancy's hand and once more laid it across the girl's nostrils and mouth.

In a moment Nancy smiled wanly. "I remember now. The ceiling fell down."

"Yes," said Helen. "It knocked you out for a few moments. I hope you're not hurt."

Miss Flora, who was still sneezing violently, insisted that they all get out of the dust at once. She began stepping across the piles of debris, with Helen helping her. When they reached the library door, the elderly woman went inside.

Helen returned to help Nancy. But by this time her friend was standing up, leaning on Aunt Rosemary's arm. She was able to make her way across the hall to the library. Aunt Rosemary suggested calling a doctor, but Nancy said this would not be necessary.

"I'm so thankful you girls weren't seriously hurt," Miss Flora said. "What a dreadful thing this is! Do you think the ghost is responsible?"

Her daughter replied at once. "No, I don't. Mother, you will recall that for some time we have had a leak in the hall whenever it rained. And the last time we had a storm, the whole ceiling was soaked. I think that weakened the plaster and it fell of its own accord."

Miss Flora remarked that a new ceiling would be a heavy expense for them. "Oh dear, more troubles all the time. But I still don't want to part with my home."

Nancy, whose faculties by now were completely restored, said with a hint of a smile, "Well, there's one worry you might not have any more, Miss Flora."

"What's that?"

"Mr. Gomber," said Nancy, "may not be so interested in buying this property when he sees what happened."

"Oh, I don't know," Aunt Rosemary spoke up. "He's pretty persistent."

Nancy said she felt all right now and suggested that she and Helen start cleaning up the hall.

Miss Flora would not hear of this. "Rosemary and I are going to help," she said determinedly.

Cartons were brought from the cellar and one after the other was filled with the debris. After it had all been carried outdoors, mops and dust cloths were brought into use. Within an hour all the gritty plaster dust had been removed.

The weary workers had just finished their job when the telephone rang. Nancy, being closest to the instrument, answered it. Hannah Gruen was calling.

"Nancy! What happened?" she asked. "I've

been waiting over an hour for you to call me back. What's the matter?"

Nancy gave her all the details.

"What's going to happen to you next?" the housekeeper exclaimed.

The young sleuth laughed. "Something good. I hope."

She asked Hannah to look for her copy of the *River Heights Gazette* of the Tuesday before. In a few minutes the housekeeper brought it to the phone and Nancy asked her to turn to page fourteen. "That has the classified ads," she said. "Now tell me what the ad is right in the center of the page."

"Do you mean the one about used cars?"

"That must be it," Nancy replied. "That's not in my paper."

Hannah Gruen said it was an ad for Aken's, a used-car dealer. "He's at 24 Main Street in Hancock."

"And now turn the page and tell me what ad is on the back of it," Nancy requested.

"It's a story about a school picnic," Hannah told her. "Does either one of them help you?"

"Yes, Hannah, I believe you've given me just the information I wanted. This may prove to be valuable. Thanks a lot."

After Nancy had finished the call, she started to dial police headquarters, then changed her mind. The ghost might be hiding somewhere in the

house to listen—or if he had installed microphones at various points, any conversations could
be picked up and recorded on a machine a distance
away.

"It would be wiser for me to discuss the whole
matter in person with the police, I'm sure," Nancy
decided.

Divulging her destination only to Helen, she
told the others she was going to drive downtown
but would not be gone long.

"You're sure you feel able?" Aunt Rosemary
asked her.

"I'm perfectly fine," Nancy insisted.

She set off in the convertible, hopeful that
through the clue of the used-car dealer, the police
might be able to pick up the name of one of the
suspects.

"They can track him down and through the man
locate my father!"

CHAPTER XIV

An Urgent Message

"Excellent!" Captain Rossland said after Nancy had told her story. He smiled. "The way you're building up clues, if you were on my force, I'd recommend a citation for you!"

The young sleuth smiled and thanked him. "I must find my father," she said earnestly.

"I'll call Captain McGinnis of the River Heights force at once," the officer told her. "Why don't you sit down here and wait? It shouldn't take long for them to get information from Aken's used-car lot."

Nancy agreed and took a chair in a corner of the captain's office. Presently he called to her.

"I have your answer, Miss Drew."

She jumped up and went over to his desk. The officer told her that Captain McGinnis in River Heights had been most co-operative. He had sent two men at once to Aken's used-car lot. They had just returned with a report.

"Day before yesterday an athletic-looking man with a crinkly ear came there and purchased a car. He showed a driver's license stating that he was Samuel Greenman from Huntsville."

Nancy was excited over the information. "Then it will be easy to pick him up, won't it?" she asked.

"I'm afraid not," Captain Rossland replied. "McGinnis learned from the Huntsville police that although Greenman is supposed to live at the address he gave, he is reported to have been out of town for some time."

"Then no one knows where he is?"

"Not any of his neighbors."

The officer also reported that Samuel Greenman was a person of questionable character. He was wanted on a couple of robbery charges, and police in several states had been alerted to be on the lookout for him.

"Well, if the man I saw at my car is Samuel Greenman, then maybe he's hiding in this area."

Captain Rossland smiled. "Are you going to suggest next that he is the ghost at Twin Elms?"

"Who knows?" Nancy countered.

"In any case," Captain Rossland said, "your idea that he may be hiding out around here is a good one."

Nancy was about to ask the officer another question when his phone rang. A moment later he said, "It's for you, Miss Drew."

The girl detective picked up the receiver and said, "Hello." The caller was Helen Corning and her voice sounded frantic.

"Oh, Nancy, something dreadful has happened here! You must come home at once!"

"What it it?" Nancy cried out, but Helen had already put down the instrument at her end.

Nancy told Captain Rossland of the urgent request and said she must leave at once.

"Let me know if you need the police," the officer called after her.

"Thank you, I will."

Nancy drove to Twin Elms as fast as the law allowed. As she pulled up in front of the house, she was startled to see a doctor's car there. Someone had been taken ill!

Helen met her friend at the front door. "Nancy," she said in a whisper, "Miss Flora may have had a heart attack!"

"How terrible!" Nancy said, shocked. "Tell me all about it."

"Dr. Morrison wants Miss Flora to go to the hospital right away, but she refuses. She says she won't leave here."

Helen said that the physician was still upstairs attending her great-grandmother.

"When did she become ill?" Nancy asked. "Did something in particular bring on the attack?"

Helen nodded. "Yes. It was very frightening. Miss Flora, Aunt Rosemary, and I were in the kitchen talking about supper. They wanted to have a special dish to surprise you, because they knew you were dreadfully upset."

"That was sweet of them," Nancy remarked. "Please go on, Helen."

"Miss Flora became rather tired and Aunt Rosemary suggested that she go upstairs and lie down. She had just started up the stairway, when, for some unknown reason, she turned to look back. There, in the parlor, stood a man!"

"A caller?" Nancy questioned.

"Oh, no!" Helen replied. "Miss Flora said he was an ugly, horrible-looking person. He was unshaven and his hair was kind of long."

"Do you think he was the ghost?" Nancy inquired.

"Miss Flora thought so. Well, she didn't scream. You know, she's really terribly brave. She just decided to go down and meet him herself. And then, what do you think?"

"I could guess any number of things," Nancy replied. "What did happen?"

Helen said that when Mrs. Turnbull had reached the parlor, no one was in it! "And there was no secret door open."

"What did Miss Flora do then?" Nancy asked.

"She fainted."

At this moment a tall, slender, gray-haired man, carrying a physician's bag, walked down the stairs to the front hall. Helen introduced Nancy to him, then asked about the patient.

"Well, fortunately, Miss Flora is going to be all right," said Dr. Morrison. "She is an amazing woman. With complete rest and nothing more to worry her, I believe she will be all right. In fact, she may be able to be up for short periods by this time tomorrow."

"Oh, I'm so relieved," said Helen. "I'm terribly fond of my great-grandmother and I don't want anything to happen to her."

The physician smiled. "I'll do all I can, but you people will have to help."

"How can we do that?" Nancy asked quickly.

The physician said that no one was to talk about the ghost. "Miss Flora says that she saw a man in the parlor and that he must have come in by some secret entrance. Now you know, as well as I do, that such a thing is not plausible."

"But the man couldn't have entered this house any other way," Helen told him quickly. "Every window and door on this first floor is kept locked."

The doctor raised his eyebrows. "You've heard of hallucinations?" he asked.

Nancy and Helen frowned, but remained silent.

They were sure that Miss Flora had not had an hallucination. If she had said there was a man in the parlor, then one had been there!

"Call me if you need me before tomorrow morning," the doctor said as he moved toward the front door. "Otherwise I'll drop in some time before twelve."

After the medic had left, the two girls exchanged glances. Nancy said, "Are you game to search the parlor again?"

"You bet I am," Helen responded. "Shall we start now or wait until after supper?"

Although Nancy was eager to begin at once, she thought that first she should go upstairs and extend her sympathy to Miss Flora. She also felt that a delay in serving her supper while the search went on might upset the ill woman. Helen offered to go into the kitchen at once and start preparing the meal. Nancy nodded and went up the steps.

Miss Flora had been put to bed in her daughter's room to avoid any further scares from the ghost, who seemed to operate in the elderly woman's own room.

"Miss Flora, I'm so sorry you have to stay in bed," said Nancy, walking up and smiling at the patient.

"Well, I am too," Mrs. Turnbull replied. "And I think it's a lot of nonsense. Everybody faints once in a while. If you'd ever seen what I did—that horrible face!"

"Mother!" pleaded Aunt Rosemary, who was seated in a chair on the other side of the bed. "You know what the doctor said."

"Oh, these doctors!" her mother said pettishly. "Anyway, Nancy, I'm sure I saw the ghost. Now you just look for a man who hasn't shaved in goodness knows how long and has an ugly face and kind of longish hair."

It was on the tip of Nancy's tongue to ask for information on the man's height and size, but recalling the doctor's warning, she said nothing about this. Instead, she smiled and taking one of Miss Flora's hands in her own, said:

"Let's not talk any more about this until you're up and well. Then I'll put you on the Drew and Company detective squad!"

The amusing remark made the elderly woman smile and she promised to try getting some rest.

"But first I want something to eat," she demanded. "Do you think you girls can manage alone? I'd like Rosemary to stay here with me."

"Of course we can manage, and we'll bring you exactly what you should have to eat."

Nancy went downstairs and set up a tray for Miss Flora. On it was a cup of steaming chicken bouillon, a thin slice of well-toasted bread, and a saucer of plain gelatin.

A few minutes later Helen took another tray upstairs with a more substantial meal on it for Aunt Rosemary. Then the two girls sat down in the dining room to have their own supper. After finishing it, they quickly washed and dried all the dishes, then started for the parlor.

"Where do you think we should look?" Helen whispered.

During the past half hour Nancy had been going over in her mind what spot in the parlor they might have overlooked—one which could possibly have an opening behind it. She had decided on a large cabinet built into the wall. It contained a beautiful collection of figurines, souvenirs from many places, and knickknacks of various kinds.

"I'm going to look for a hidden spring that may move the cabinet away from the wall," Nancy told Helen in a low voice.

For the first time she noticed that each of the figurines and knickknacks were set in small depressions on the shelves. Nancy wondered excitedly if this had been done so that the figurines would not fall over in case the cabinet were moved.

Eagerly she began to look on the back wall of the interior of the cabinet for a spring. She and Helen together searched every inch of the upper part but found no spring to move the great built-in piece of furniture.

On the lower part of the cabinet were two doors which Nancy had already opened many times. But then she had been looking for a large opening.

Now she was hoping to locate a tiny spring or movable panel.

Helen searched the left side, while Nancy took the right. Suddenly her pulse quickened in anticipation. She had felt a spot slightly higher than the rest.

Nancy ran her fingers back and forth across the area which was about half an inch high and three inches long.

"It may conceal something," she thought, and pushed gently against the wood.

Nancy felt a vibration in the whole cabinet.

"Helen! I've found something!" she whispered hoarsely. "Better stand back!"

Nancy pressed harder. This time the right side of the cabinet began to move forward. Nancy jumped up from her knees and stood back with Helen. Slowly, very slowly, one end of the cabinet began to move into the parlor, the other into an open space behind it.

Helen grabbed Nancy's hand in fright. What were they going to find in the secret passageway?

CHAPTER XV

A New Suspect

THE GREAT crystal chandelier illuminated the narrow passageway behind the cabinet. It was not very long. No one was in it and the place was dusty and filled with cobwebs.

"There's probably an exit at the other end of this," said Nancy. "Let's see where it goes."

"I think I'd better wait here, Nancy," Helen suggested. "This old cabinet might suddenly start to close itself. If it does, I'll yell so you can get out in time."

Nancy laughed. "You're a real pal, Helen."

As Nancy walked along the passageway, she looked carefully at the two walls which lined it. There was no visible exit from either of the solid, plastered walls. The far end, too, was solid, but this wall had been built of wood.

Nancy felt it might have some significance. At the moment she could not figure it out and started to return to the parlor. Halfway along the narrow corridor, she saw a folded piece of paper lying on the floor.

"This may prove something," she told herself eagerly, picking it up.

Just as Nancy stepped back into the parlor, Aunt Rosemary appeared. She stared in astonishment at the opening in the wall and at the cabinet which now stood at right angles to it.

"You found something?" she asked.

"Only this," Nancy replied, and handed Aunt Rosemary the folded paper.

As the girls looked over her shoulder, Mrs. Hayes opened it. "This is an unfinished letter," she commented, then started to decipher the old-fashioned handwriting. "Why, this was written way back in 1785—not long after the house was built."

The note read:

My honorable friend Benjamin:

The disloyalty of two of my servants has just come to my attention. I am afraid they plan to harm the cause of the Colonies. I will have them properly punished. My good fortune in learning about this disloyalty came while I was at my listening post. Every word spoken in the servants' sitting room can be overheard by me.

I will watch for further—

The letter ended at this point. Instantly Helen said, "Listening post?"

"It must be at the end of this passageway," Nancy guessed. "Aunt Rosemary, what room would connect with it?"

"I presume the kitchen," Mrs. Hayes replied. "And it seems to me that I once heard that the present kitchen was a sitting room for the servants long ago. You recall that back in Colonial days food was never cooked in a mansion. It was always prepared in another building and brought in on great trays."

Helen smiled. "With a listening post the poor servants here didn't have a chance for a good chit-chat together. Their conversations were never a secret from their master!"

Nancy and Aunt Rosemary smiled too and nodded, then the young sleuth said, "Let's see if this listening post still works."

It was arranged that Helen would go into the kitchen and start talking. Nancy would stand at the end of the corridor to listen. Aunt Rosemary, who was shown how to work the hidden spring on the cabinet, would act as guard if the great piece of furniture suddenly started to move and close the opening.

"All ready?" Helen asked. She moved out of the room.

When she thought Nancy was at her post, she

began to talk about her forthcoming wedding and asked Nancy to be in the bridal party.

"I can hear Helen very plainly!" Nancy called excitedly to Aunt Rosemary. "The listening post is as good as ever!"

When the test was over, and the cabinet manually closed by Nancy, she and Helen and Aunt Rosemary held a whispered conversation. They all decided that the ghost knew about the passageway and had overheard plans which those in the house were making. Probably this was where the ghost disappeared after Miss Flora spotted him.

"Funny that we seem to do more planning while we're in the kitchen than in any other room," Aunt Rosemary remarked.

Helen said she wondered if this listening post was unique with the owner and architect of Twin Elms mansion.

"No, indeed," Aunt Rosemary told her. "Many old homes where there were servants had such places. Don't forget that our country has been involved in several wars, during which traitors and spies found it easy to get information while posing as servants."

"Very clever," Helen remarked. "And I suppose a lot of the people who were caught never knew how they had been found out."

"No doubt," said Aunt Rosemary.

At that moment they heard Miss Flora's feeble

voice calling from the bedroom and hurried up the steps to be sure that she was all right. They found her smiling, but she complained that she did not like to stay alone so long.

"I won't leave you again tonight, Mother," Aunt Rosemary promised. "I'm going to sleep on the couch in this room so as not to disturb you. Now try to get a little sleep."

The following morning Nancy had a phone call from Hannah Gruen, whose voice sounded very irate. "I've just heard from Mr. Barradale, the railroad lawyer, Nancy. He lost your address and phone number, so he called here. I'm furious at what he had to say. He hinted that your father might be staying away on purpose because he wasn't able to produce Willie Wharton!"

Nancy was angry too. "Why, that's absolutely unfair and untrue," she cried.

"Well, I just wouldn't stand for it if I were you," Hannah Gruen stated flatly. "And that's only half of it."

"You mean he had more to say about Dad?" Nancy questioned quickly.

"No, not that," the housekeeper answered. "He was calling to say that the railroad can't hold up the bridge project any longer. If some new evidence isn't produced by Monday, the railroad will be forced to accede to the demands of Willie Wharton and all those other property owners!"

"Oh, that would be a great blow to Dad!" said

Nancy. "He wouldn't want this to happen. He's sure that the signature on that contract of sale is Willie Wharton's. All he has to do is find him and prove it."

"Everything is such a mess," said Mrs. Gruen. "I was talking to the police just before I called you and they have no leads at all to where your father might be."

"Hannah, this is dreadful!" said Nancy. "I don't know how, but I intend to find Dad—and quickly, too!"

After the conversation between herself and the housekeeper was over, Nancy walked up and down the hall, as she tried to formulate a plan. Something must be done!

Suddenly Nancy went to the front door, opened it, and walked outside. She breathed deeply of the lovely morning air and headed for the rose garden. She let the full beauty of the estate sink into her consciousness, before permitting herself to think further about the knotty problem before her.

Long ago Mr. Drew had taught Nancy that the best way to clear one's brain is to commune with Nature for a time. Nancy went up one walk and down another, listening to the twittering of the birds and now and then the song of the meadow lark. Again she smelled deeply of the roses and the sweet wisteria which hung over a sagging arbor.

Ten minutes later she returned to the house and sat down on the porch steps. Almost at once a mental image of Nathan Gomber came to her as clearly as if the man had been standing in front of her. The young sleuth's mind began to put together the various pieces of the puzzle regarding him and the railroad property.

"Maybe Nathan Gomber is keeping Willie Wharton away!" she said to herself. "Willie may even be a prisoner! And if Gomber is that kind of a person, maybe he engineered the abduction of my father!"

The very thought frightened Nancy. Leaping up, she decided to ask the police to have Nathan Gomber shadowed.

"I'll go down to headquarters and talk to Captain Rossland," she decided. "And I'll ask Helen to go along. The cleaning woman is here, so she can help Aunt Rosemary in case of an emergency."

Without explaining her real purpose in wanting to go downtown, Nancy merely asked Helen to accompany her there for some necessary marketing. The two girls drove off, and on the way to town Nancy gave Helen full details of her latest theories about Nathan Gomber.

Helen was amazed. "And here he was acting so worried about your father's safety!"

When the girls reached police headquarters, they had to wait a few minutes to see Captain Rossland. Nancy fidgeted under the delay. Every moment seemed doubly precious now.   But finally the girls were ushered inside and the officer greeted them warmly.

"Another clue, Miss Drew?" he asked with a smile.

Nancy told her story quickly.

"I think you're on the right track," the officer stated. "I'll be very glad to get in touch with your Captain McGinnis in River Heights and relay your message. And I'll notify all the men on my force to be on the lookout for this Nathan Gomber."

"Thank you," said Nancy gratefully. "Every hour that goes by I become more and more worried about my father."

"A break should come soon," the officer told her kindly. "The minute I hear anything I'll let you know."

Nancy thanked him and the girls went on their way. It took every bit of Nancy's stamina not to show her inmost feelings. She rolled the cart through the supermarket almost automatically, picking out needed food items. Her mind would say, "We need more canned peas because the ghost took what we had," and at the meat counter she reflected, "Dad loves thick, juicy steaks."

Finally the marketing was finished and the packages stowed in the rear of the convertible. On the way home, Helen asked Nancy what plans she had for pursuing the mystery.

"To tell the truth, I've been thinking about it continuously, but so far I haven't come up with any new ideas," Nancy answered. "I'm sure, though, that something will pop up."

When the girls were a little distance from the entrance to the Twin Elms estate, they saw a car suddenly pull out of the driveway and make a right turn. The driver leaned out his window and looked back. He wore a smug grin.

"Why, it's Nathan Gomber!" Nancy cried out.

"And did you see that smirk on his face?" Helen asked. "Oh, Nancy, maybe that means he's finally persuaded Miss Flora to sell the property to him!"

"Yes," Nancy replied grimly. "And also, here I've just asked the police to shadow him and I'm the first person to see him!"

With that Nancy put on speed and shot ahead. As she passed the driveway to the estate, Helen asked, "Where are you going?"

"I'm following Nathan Gomber until I catch him!"

CHAPTER XVI

Sold!

"OH, NANCY, I hope we meet a police officer!" said Helen Corning. "If Gomber is a kidnaper, he may try to harm us if we do catch up to him!"

"We'll have to be cautious," Nancy admitted. "But I'm afraid we're not going to meet any policeman. I haven't seen one on these roads in all the time I've been here."

Both girls watched the car ahead of them intently. It was near enough for Nancy to be able to read the license number. She wondered if the car was registered under Gomber's name or someone else's. If it belonged to a friend of his, this fact might lead the police to another suspect.

"Where do you think Gomber's going?" Helen asked presently. "To meet somebody?"

"Perhaps. And he may be on his way back to River Heights."

"Not yet," Helen said, for at that moment Gomber had reached a crossroads and turned sharp right. "That road leads away from River Heights."

"But it does lead past Riverview Manor," Nancy replied tensely as she neared the crossroads.

Turning right, the girls saw Gomber ahead, tearing along at a terrific speed. He passed the vacant mansion. A short distance beyond it he began to turn his car lights off and on.

"What's he doing that for?" Helen queried. "Is he just testing his lights?"

Nancy was not inclined to think so. "I believe he's signaling to someone. Look all around, Helen, and see if you can spot anybody." She herself was driving so fast that she did not dare take her eyes from the road.

Helen gazed right and left, and then turned to gaze through the back window. "I don't see a soul," she reported.

Nancy began to feel uneasy. It was possible that Gomber might have been signaling to someone to follow the girls. "Helen, keep looking out the rear window and see if a car appears and starts to follow us."

"Maybe we ought to give up the chase and just tell the police about Gomber," Helen said a bit fearfully.

But Nancy did not want to do this. "I think it will help us a lot to know where he's heading."

She continued the pursuit and several miles farther on came to the town of Hancock.

"Isn't this where that crinkly-eared fellow lives?" Helen inquired.

"Yes."

"Then it's my guess Gomber is going to see him."

Nancy reminded her friend that the man was reported to be out of town, presumably because he was wanted by the police on a couple of robbery charges.

Though Hancock was small, there was a great deal of traffic on the main street. In the center of town at an intersection, there was a signal light. Gomber shot through the green, but by the time Nancy reached the spot, the light had turned red.

"Oh dear!" she fumed. "Now I'll probably lose him!"

In a few seconds the light changed to green and Nancy again took up her pursuit. But she felt that at this point it was futile. Gomber could have turned down any of a number of side streets, or if he had gone straight through the town he would now be so far ahead of her that it was doubtful she could catch him. Nancy went on, nevertheless, for another three miles. Then, catching no sight of her quarry, she decided to give up the chase.

"I guess it's hopeless, Helen," she said. "I'm going back to Hancock and report everything to the police there. I'll ask them to get in touch with Captain Rossland and Captain McGinnis."

"Oh, I hope they capture Gomber!" Helen

said. "He's such a horrible man! He ought to be put in jail just for his bad manners!"

Smiling, Nancy turned the car and headed back for Hancock. A woman passer-by gave her directions to police headquarters and a few moments later Nancy parked in front of it. The girls went inside the building. Nancy told the officer in charge who they were, then gave him full details of the recent chase.

The officer listened attentively, then said, "I'll telephone your River Heights captain first."

"And please alert your own men and the State Police," Nancy requested.

He nodded. "Don't worry, Miss Drew, I'll follow through from here." He picked up his phone.

Helen urged Nancy to leave immediately. "While you were talking, I kept thinking about Gomber's visit to Twin Elms. I have a feeling something may have happened there. You remember what a self-satisfied look Gomber had on his face when we saw him come out of the driveway."

"You're right," Nancy agreed. "We'd better hurry back there."

It was a long drive back to Twin Elms and the closer the girls go to it, the more worried they became. "Miss Flora was already ill," Helen said tensely, "and Gomber's visit may have made her worse."

On reaching the house, the front door was opened by Aunt Rosemary, who looked pale.

"I'm so glad you've returned," she said. "My mother is much worse. She has had a bad shock. I'm waiting for Dr. Morrison."

Mrs. Hayes' voice was trembling and she found it hard to go on. Nancy said sympathetically, "We know Nathan Gomber was here. We've been chasing his car, but lost it. Did he upset Miss Flora?"

"Yes. I was out of the house about twenty minutes talking with the gardener and didn't happen to see Gomber drive up. The cleaning woman, Lillie, let him in. Of course she didn't know who he was and thought he was all right. When she finally came outside to tell me, I had walked way over to the wisteria arbor at the far end of the grounds.

"In the meantime, Gomber went upstairs. He began talking to Mother about selling the mansion. When she refused, he threatened her, saying that if she did not sign, all kinds of dreadful things would happen to me and to both you girls.

"Poor mother couldn't hold out any longer. At this moment Lillie, who couldn't find me, returned and went upstairs. She actually witnessed Mother's signature on the contract of sale and signed her own name to it. So Gomber has won!"

Aunt Rosemary sank into the chair by the telephone and began to cry. Nancy and Helen put their arms around her, but before either could say a word of comfort, they heard a car drive up in front of the mansion. At once Mrs. Hayes dried her eyes and said, "It must be Dr. Morrison."

Nancy opened the door and admitted the physician. The whole group went upstairs where Miss Flora lay staring at the ceiling like someone in a trance. She was murmuring:

"I shouldn't have signed! I shouldn't have sold Twin Elms!"

Dr. Morrison took the patient's pulse and listened to her heartbeat with a stethoscope. A few moments later he said, "Mrs. Turnbull, won't you please let me take you to the hospital?"

"Not yet," said Miss Flora stubbornly. She smiled wanly. "I know I'm ill. But I'm not going to get better any quicker in the hospital than I am right here. I'll be moving out of Twin Elms soon enough and I want to stay here as long as I can. Oh, why did I ever sign my name to that paper?"

As an expression of defeat came over the physician's face, Nancy moved to the bedside. "Miss Flora," she said gently, "maybe the deal will never go through. In the first place, perhaps we can prove that you signed under coercion. If that doesn't work, you know it takes a long time to have a title search made on property. By then, maybe Gomber will change his mind."

"Oh, I hope you're right," the elderly woman replied, squeezing Nancy's hand affectionately.

The girls left the room, so that Dr. Morrison could examine the patient further and prescribe for her. They decided to say nothing of their morning's adventure to Miss Flora, but at luncheon they gave Aunt Rosemary a full account.

"I'm almost glad you didn't catch Gomber." Mrs. Hayes exclaimed. "He might have harmed you both."

Nancy said she felt sure that the police of one town or the other would soon capture him, and then perhaps many things could be explained. "For one, we can find out why he was turning his lights off and on. I have a hunch he was signaling to someone and that the person was hidden in Riverview Manor!"

"You may be right," Aunt Rosemary replied.

Helen suddenly leaned across the table. "Do you suppose our ghost thief hides out there?"

"I think it's very probable," Nancy answered. "I'd like to do some sleuthing in that old mansion."

"You're not going to break in?" Helen asked, horrified.

Her friend smiled. "No, Helen, I'm not going to evade the law. I'll go to the realtor who is handling the property and ask him to show me the place. Want to come along?"

Helen shivered a little but said she was game. "Let's do it this afternoon."

"Oh dear." Aunt Rosemary gave an anxious

sigh. "I don't know whether or not I should let you. It sounds very dangerous to me."

"If the realtor is with us, we should be safe," Helen spoke up. Her aunt then gave her consent, and added that the realtor, Mr. Dodd, had an office on Main Street.

Conversation ceased for a few moments as the threesome finished luncheon. They had just left the table when they heard a loud thump upstairs.

"Oh, goodness!" Aunt Rosemary cried out. "I hope Mother hasn't fallen!"

She and the girls dashed up the stairs. Miss Flora was in bed, but she was trembling like a leaf in the wind. She pointed a thin, white hand toward the ceiling.

"It was up in the attic! Sombody's there!"

CHAPTER XVII

Through the Trap Door

"LET's find out who's in the attic!" Nancy urged as she ran from the room, Helen at her heels.

"Mother, will you be all right if I leave you a few moments?" Aunt Rosemary asked. "I'd like to go with the girls."

"Of course. Run along."

Nancy and Helen were already on their way to the third floor. They did not bother to go noiselessly, but raced up the center of the creaking stairs. Reaching the attic, they lighted two of the candles and looked around. They saw no one, and began to look behind trunks and pieces of furniture. Nobody was hiding.

"And there's no evidence," said Nancy, "that the alarming thump was caused by a falling box or carton."

"There's only one answer," Helen decided. "The ghost *was* here. But how did he get in?"

The words were scarcely out of her mouth when the group heard a man's spine-chilling laugh. It had not come from downstairs.

"He—he's back of the wall!" Helen gasped fearfully. Nancy agreed, but Aunt Rosemary said, "That laugh could have come from the roof."

Helen looked at her aunt questioningly. "You —you mean that the ghost swings onto the roof from a tree and climbs in here somehow?"

"I think it very likely," her aunt replied. "My father once told my mother that there's a trap door to the roof. I never saw it and I forgot having heard of it until this minute."

Holding their candles high, the girls examined every inch of the peaked, beamed ceiling. The rafters were set close together with wood panels between them.

"I see something that might be a trap door!" Nancy called out presently from near one end of the attic. She showed the others where some short panels formed an almost perfect square.

"But how does it open?" Helen asked. "There's no knob or hook or any kind of gadget to grab hold of."

"It might have been removed, or rusted off," Nancy said.

She asked Helen to help her drag a high wooden box across the floor until it was directly under the suspected section and Nancy stepped up onto it. Focusing her light on the four edges of the panels, the young sleuth finally discovered a piece of metal wedged between two of the planks.

"I think I see a way to open this," Nancy said, "but I'll need some tools."

"I'll get the ones I found before," Helen offered. She hurried downstairs and procured them. Nancy tried one tool after another, but none would work; they were either too wide to fit into the crack or they would not budge the piece of metal either up or down.

Nancy looked down at Aunt Rosemary. "Do you happen to have an old-fashioned buttonhook?" she asked. "That might be just the thing for this job."

"Indeed I have—in fact, Mother has several of them. I'll get one."

Aunt Rosemary was gone only a few minutes. Upon her return, she handed Nancy a long, silver-handled buttonhook inscribed with Mrs. Turnbull's initials. "Mother used this to fasten her high button shoes. She has a smaller matching one for glove buttons. In olden days," she told the girls, "no lady's gloves were the pull-on type. They all had buttons."

Nancy inserted the long buttonhook into the ceiling crack and almost at once was able to grasp the piece of metal and pull it down. Now she began tugging on it. When nothing happened, Helen climbed up on the box beside her friend and helped pull.

Presently there was a groaning, rasping noise and the square section of the ceiling began to move downward. The girls continued to yank on the metal piece and slowly a folded ladder attached to the wood became visible.

"The trap door's up there!" Helen cried gleefully, looking at the roof. "Nancy, you shall have the honor of being the first one to look out."

Nancy smiled. "And, you mean, capture the ghost?"

As the ladder was straightened out, creaking with each pull, and set against the roof, Nancy felt sure, however, that the ghost did not use it. The ladder made entirely too much noise! She also doubted that he was on the roof, but it would do no harm to look. She might pick up a clue of some sort!

"Well, here I go," Nancy said, and started to ascend the rungs.

When she reached the top, Nancy unfastened the trap door and shoved it upward. She poked her head outdoors and looked around. No one was in sight on the roof, but in the center stood a circular wooden lookout. It occurred to Nancy that possibly the ghost might be hiding in it!

She called down to Aunt Rosemary and Helen to look up at the attic ceiling for evidence of an opening into the tower. They returned to Nancy in half a minute to report that they could find no sign of another trap door.

"There probably was one in olden days," said Aunt Rosemary, "but it was closed up."

A sudden daring idea came to the girl detective. "I'm going to crawl over to that lookout and see if anybody's in it!" she told the two below.

Before either of them could object, she started to crawl along the ridgepole above the wooden shingled sides of the deeply slanting roof. Helen had raced up the ladder, and now watched her friend fearfully.

"Be careful, Nancy!" she warned.

Nancy was doing just that. She must keep a perfect balance or tumble down to almost certain death. Halfway to the tower, the daring girl began to feel that she had been foolhardy, but she was determined to reach her goal.

"Only five more feet to go," Nancy told herself presently.

With a sigh of relief, she reached the tower and pulled herself up. It was circular and had openings on each side. She looked in. No "ghost"!

Nancy decided to step inside the opening and examine the floor. She set one foot down, but immediately the boards, rotted from the weather, gave way beneath her.

"It's a good thing I didn't put my whole weight on it," she thought thankfully.

"Do you see anything?" Helen called.

"Not a thing. This floor hasn't been in use for a long time."

"Then the ghost didn't come in by way of the roof," Helen stated.

Nancy nodded in agreement. "The only places left to look are the chimneys," the young sleuth told her friend. "I'll check them."

There were four of these and Nancy crawled to each one in turn. She looked inside but found nothing to suggest that the ghost used any of them for entry.

Balancing herself against the last chimney, Nancy surveyed the countryside around her. What a beautiful and picturesque panorama it was,

she thought! Not far away was a lazy little river, whose waters sparkled in the sunlight. The surrounding fields were green and sprinkled with patches of white daisies.

Nancy looked down on the grounds of Twin Elms and tried in her mind to reconstruct the original landscaping.

"That brick walk to the next property must

have had a lovely boxwood hedge at one time," she said to herself.

Her gaze now turned to Riverview Manor. The grounds there were overgrown with weeds and several shutters were missing from the house. Suddenly Nancy's attention was drawn to one of the uncovered windowpanes. Did she see a light moving inside?

It disappeared a moment later and Nancy could not be sure. Perhaps the sun shining on the glass had created an optical illusion.

"Still, somebody just might be in that house," the young sleuth thought. "The sooner I get over there and see what I can find out, the better! If the ghost is hiding out there, maybe he uses some underground passage from one of the outbuildings on the property."

She crawled cautiously back to the trap door and together the girls closed it. Aunt Rosemary had already gone downstairs to take care of her mother.

Nancy told Helen what she thought she had just seen in the neighboring mansion. "I'll change my clothes right away. Then let's go see Mr. Dodd, the realtor broker for Riverview Manor."

A half hour later the two girls walked into the real-estate office. Mr. Dodd himself was there and Nancy asked him about looking at Riverview Manor.

"I'm sorry, miss," he said, "but the house has just been sold."

Nancy was stunned. She could see all her plans crumbling into nothingness. Then a thought came to her. Perhaps the new owner would not object if she looked around, anyway.

"Would you mind telling me, Mr. Dodd, who purchased Riverview Manor?"

"Not at all," the realtor replied. "A man named Nathan Gomber."

CHAPTER XVIII

A Confession

NANCY DREW'S face wore such a disappointed look that Mr. Dodd, the realtor, said kindly, "Don't take it so hard, miss. I don't think you'd be particularly interested in Riverview Manor. It's really not in very good condition. Besides, you'd need a pile of money to fix that place up."

Without commenting on his statement, Nancy asked, "Couldn't you possibly arrange for me to see the inside of the mansion?"

Mr. Dodd shook his head. "I'm afraid Mr. Gomber wouldn't like that."

Nancy was reluctant to give up. Why, her father might even be a prisoner in that very house! "Of course I can report my suspicion to the police," the young sleuth thought.

She decided to wait until morning. Then, if there was still no news of Mr. Drew, she would pass along the word to Captain Rossland.

Mr. Dodd's telephone rang. As he answered it, Nancy and Helen started to leave his office. But he immediately waved them back.

"The call is from Chief Rossland, Miss Drew," he said. "He phoned Twin Elms and learned you were here. He wants to see you at once."

"Thank you," said Nancy, and the girls left. They hurried to police headquarters, wondering why the officer wanted to speak to Nancy.

"Oh, if only it's news of Dad," she exclaimed fervently. "But why didn't he get in touch with me himself?"

"I don't want to be a killjoy," Helen spoke up. "But maybe it's not about your father at all. Perhaps they've caught Nathan Gomber."

Nancy parked in front of headquarters and the two girls hurried inside the building. Captain Rossland was expecting them and they were immediately ushered into his office. Nancy introduced Helen Corning.

"I won't keep you in suspense," the officer said, watching Nancy's eager face. "We have arrested Samuel Greenman!"

"The crinkly-eared man?" Helen asked.

"That's right," Captain Rossland replied. "Thanks to your tip about the used car, Miss Drew, our men had no trouble at all locating him."

The officer went on to say, however, that the prisoner refused to confess that he had had anything to do with Mr. Drew's disappearance.

"Furthermore, Harry the taxi driver—we have him here—insists that he cannot positively identify Greenman as one of the passengers in his cab. We believe Harry is scared that Greenman's pals will beat him up or attack members of his family."

"Harry did tell me," Nancy put in, "that his passenger had threatened harm to his family unless he forgot all about what he had seen."

"That proves our theory," Captain Rossland stated with conviction. "Miss Drew, we think you can help the police."

"I'll be glad to.   How?"

Captain Rossland smiled. "You may not know it, but you're a very persuasive young lady.   I believe that you might be able to get information out of both Harry and Greenman, where we have failed."

After a moment's thought, Nancy replied modestly, "I'll be happy to try, but on one condition."   She grinned at the officer.   "I must talk to these men alone."

"Request granted."   Captain Rossland smiled. He added that he and Helen would wait outside and he would have Harry brought in.

"Good luck," said Helen as she and the captain left the room.

A few moments later Harry walked in alone. "Oh hello, miss," he said to Nancy, barely raising his eyes from the floor.

"Won't you sit down, Harry," Nancy asked, indicating a chair alongside hers. "It was nice of the captain to let me talk to you."

Harry seated himself, but said nothing. He twisted his driver's cap nervously in his hands and kept his gaze downward.

"Harry," Nancy began, "I guess your children would feel terrible if you were kidnaped."

"It would cut 'em to pieces," the cabman stated emphatically.

"Then you know how I feel," Nancy went on. "Not a word from my father for two whole days. If your children knew somebody who'd seen the person who kidnaped you, wouldn't they feel bad if the man wouldn't talk?"

Harry at last raised his eyes and looked straight at Nancy. "I get you, miss. When somethin' comes home to you, it makes all the difference in the world. You win! I *can* identify that scoundrel Greenman, and I will. Call the captain in."

Nancy did not wait a second. She opened the door and summoned the officer.

"Harry has something to tell you," Nancy said to Captain Rossland.

"Yeah," said Harry, "I'm not goin' to hold out any longer. I admit Greenman had me scared, but he's the guy who rode in my cab, then ordered me to keep my mouth shut after that other passenger blacked out."

Captain Rossland looked astounded. It was evident he could hardly believe that Nancy in only a few minutes had persuaded the man to talk!

"And now," Nancy asked, "may I talk to your prisoner?"

"I'll have you taken to his cell," the captain responded, and rang for a guard.

Nancy was led down a corridor, past a row of cells until they came to one where the man with the crinkled ear sat on a cot.

"Greenman," said the guard, "step up here. This is Miss Nancy Drew, daughter of the kidnaped man. She wants to talk to you."

The prisoner shuffled forward, but mumbled, "I ain't goin' to answer no questions."

Nancy waited until the guard had moved off, then she smiled at the prisoner. "We all make mistakes at times," she said. "We're often misled by people who urge us to do things we shouldn't. Maybe you're afraid you'll receive the death sentence for helping to kidnap my father. But if you didn't realize the seriousness of the whole thing, the complaint against you may turn out just to be conspiracy."

To Nancy's astonishment, Greenman suddenly burst out, "You've got me exactly right, miss. I had almost nothing to do with takin' your father away. The guy I was with—*he's* the old-timer. He's got a long prison record. I haven't. Honest, miss, this is my first offense.

"I'll tell you the whole story. I met this guy

only Monday night. He sure sold me a bill of goods. But all I did was see that your pop didn't run away. The old-timer's the one that drugged him."

"Where is my father now?" Nancy interrupted.

"I don't know. Honest I don't," Greenman insisted. "Part of the plan was for somebody to follow the taxi. After a while Mr. Drew was to be given a whiff of somethin'. It didn't have no smell. That's why our taxi driver didn't catch on. And it didn't knock the rest of us out, 'cause you have to put the stuff right under a fellow's nose to make it work."

"And the person who was following in a car and took my father away, who is he?"

"I don't know," the prisoner answered, and Nancy felt that he was telling the truth.

"Did you get any money for doing this?" Nancy asked him.

"A little. Not as much as it was worth, especially if I have to go to prison. The guy who paid us for our work was the one in the car who took your father away."

"Will you describe him?" Nancy requested.

"Sure. Hope the police catch him soon. He's in his early fifties—short and heavy-set, pale, and has kind of watery blue eyes."

Nancy asked the prisoner if he would dictate the same confession for the police and the man nodded. "And I'm awful sorry I caused all this

worry, miss. I hope you find your father soon and
I wish I could help you more. I guess I am a
coward. I'm too scared to tell the name of the
guy who talked me into this whole thing. He's
really a bad actor—no tellin' what'd happen to
me if I gave his name."

The young sleuth felt that she had obtained all
the information she possibly could from the man.
She went back to Captain Rossland, who for the
second time was amazed by the girl's success. He
called a stenographer. Then he said good-by to
Nancy and Helen and went off toward Greenman's
cell.

On the way back to Twin Elms, Helen con-
gratulated her friend. "Now that one of the kid-
napers has been caught, I'm sure that your father
will be found soon, Nancy. Who do you suppose
the man was who took your father from Greenman
and his friend?"

Nancy looked puzzled, then answered, "We
know from his description that he wasn't Gomber.
But, Helen, a hunch of mine is growing stronger
all the time that he's back of this whole thing.
And putting two and two together, I believe it
was Willie Wharton who drove that car.

"And I also believe Wharton's the one who's
been playing ghost, using masks at times—like the
gorilla and the unshaven, long-haired man.

"Somehow he gets into the mansion and listens
to conversations. He heard that I was going to be

asked to solve the mystery at Twin Elms and told
Gomber. That's why Gomber came to our home
and tried to keep me from coming here by saying
I should stick close to Dad."

"That's right," said Helen. "And when he
found that didn't work, he had Willie and Greenman and that other man kidnap your dad. He figured it would surely get you away from Twin Elms.
He wanted to scare Miss Flora into selling the
property, and he thought if you were around you
might dissuade her."

"But in that I didn't succeed," said Nancy a bit
forlornly. "Besides, they knew Dad could stop
those greedy land owners from forcing the railroad to pay them more for their property. That's
why I'm sure Gomber and Wharton won't release
him until after they get what they want."

Helen laid a hand on Nancy's shoulder. "I'm
so terribly sorry about this. What can we do
next?"

"Somehow I have a feeling, Helen," her friend
replied, "that you and I are going to find Willie
Wharton before very long. And if we do, and I
find out he really signed that contract of sale, I
want certain people to be around."

"Who?" Helen asked, puzzled.

"Mr. Barradale, the lawyer, and Mr. Watson
the notary public."

The young sleuth put her thought into action.
Knowing that Monday was the deadline set by the

railroad, she determined to do her utmost before that time to solve the complicated mystery. Back at Twin Elms, Nancy went to the telephone and put in a call to Mr. Barradale's office. She did not dare mention Gomber's or Willie Wharton's name for fear one or the other of them might be listening. She merely asked the young lawyer if he could possibly come to Cliffwood and bring with him whatever he felt was necessary for him to win his case.

"I think I understand what you really mean to say," he replied. "I take it you can't talk freely. Is that correct?"

"Yes."

"Then I'll ask the questions. You want me to come to the address that you gave us the other day?"

"Yes. About noon."

"And you'd like me to bring along the contract of sale with Willie Wharton's signature?"

"Yes. That will be fine." Nancy thanked him and hung up.

Turning from the telephone, she went to find Helen and said, "There's still lots of daylight. Even though we can't get inside Riverview Manor, we can hunt through the outbuildings over there for the entrance to an underground passage to this house."

"All right," her friend agreed. "But this time you do the searching. I'll be the lookout."

Nancy chose the old smokehouse of Riverview Manor first, since this was closest to the Twin Elms property line. It yielded no clue and she moved on to the carriage house. But neither in this building, nor any of the others, did the girl detective find any indication of entrances to an underground passageway. Finally she gave up and rejoined Helen.

"If there is an opening, it must be from inside Riverview Manor," Nancy stated. "Oh, Helen, it's exasperating not to be able to get in there!"

"I wouldn't go in there now in any case," Helen remarked. "It's way past suppertime and I'm starved. Besides, pretty soon it'll be dark."

The girls returned to Twin Elms and ate supper. A short time later someone banged the front-door knocker. Both girls went to the door. They were amazed to find that the caller was Mr. Dodd, the realtor. He held out a large brass key toward Nancy.

"What's this for?" she asked, mystified.

Mr. Dodd smiled.

"It's the front-door key to Riverview Manor. I've decided that you can look around the mansion tomorrow morning all you please."

CHAPTER XIX

The Hidden Staircase

SEEING the look of delight on Nancy's face, Mr. Dodd laughed. "Do you think that house is haunted as well as this one?" he asked. "I hear you like to solve mysteries."

"Yes, I do." Not wishing to reveal her real purpose to the realtor, the young sleuth also laughed. "Do you think I might find a ghost over there?" she countered.

"Well, I never saw one, but you never can tell," the man responded with a chuckle. He said he would leave the key with Nancy until Saturday evening and then pick it up. "If Mr. Gomber should show up in the meantime, I have a key to the kitchen door that he can use."

Nancy thanked Mr. Dodd and with a grin said she would let him know if she found a ghost at Riverview Manor.

She could hardly wait for the next morning to

arrive. Miss Flora was not told of the girls' plan to visit the neighboring house.

Immediately after breakfast, they set off for Riverview Manor. Aunt Rosemary went with them to the back door and wished the two good luck. "Promise me you won't take any chances," she begged.

"Promise," they said in unison.

With flashlights in their skirt pockets, Nancy and Helen hurried through the garden and into the grounds of Riverview Manor estate.

As they approached the front porch, Helen showed signs of nervousness. "Nancy, what will we do if we meet the ghost?" she asked.

"Just tell him we've found him out," her friend answered determinedly.

Helen said no more and watched as Nancy inserted the enormous brass key in the lock. It turned easily and the girls let themselves into the hall. Architecturally it was the same as Twin Elms mansion, but how different it looked now! The blinds were closed, lending an eerie atmosphere to the dusky interior. Dust lay everywhere, and cobwebs festooned the corners of the ceiling and spindles of the staircase.

"It certainly doesn't look as if anybody lives here," Helen remarked. "Where do we start hunting?"

"I want to take a look in the kitchen," said Nancy.

When they walked into it, Helen gasped. "I guess I was wrong. Someone has been eating here." Eggshells, several empty milk bottles, some chicken bones and pieces of waxed paper cluttered the sink.

Nancy, realizing that Helen was very uneasy, whispered to her with a giggle, "If the ghost lives here, he has a good appetite!"

The young sleuth took out her flashlight and beamed it around the floors and walls of the kitchen. There was no sign of a secret opening. As she went from room to room on the first floor, Helen followed and together they searched every inch of the place for a clue to a concealed door. At last they came to the conclusion there was none.

"You know, it could be in the cellar," Nancy suggested.

"Well, you're not going down there," Helen said firmly. "That is, not without a policeman. It's too dangerous. As for myself, I want to live to get married and not be hit over the head in the dark by that ghost, so Jim won't have a bride!"

Nancy laughed. "You win. But I'll tell you why. At the moment I am more interested in finding my father than in hunting for a secret passageway. He may be a prisoner in one of the rooms upstairs. I'm going to find out."

The door to the back stairway was unlocked and the one at the top stood open. Nancy asked

Helen to stand at the foot of the main staircase, while she herself went up the back steps. "If that ghost is up there and tries to escape, he won't be able to slip out that way," she explained.

Helen took her post in the front hall and Nancy crept up the back steps. No one tried to come down either stairs. Helen now went to the second floor and together she and Nancy began a search of the rooms. They found nothing suspicious. Mr. Drew was not there. There was no sign of a ghost. None of the walls revealed a possible secret opening. But the bedroom which corresponded to Miss Flora's had a clothes closet built in at the end next to the fireplace.

"In Colonial times closets were a rarity," Nancy remarked to Helen. "I wonder if this closet was added at that time and has any special significance."

Quickly she opened one of the large double doors and looked inside. The rear wall was formed of two very wide wooden planks. In the center was a round knob, sunk in the wood.

"This is strange," Nancy remarked excitedly.

She pulled on the knob but the wall did not move. Next, she pushed the knob down hard, leaning her full weight against the panel.

Suddenly the wall pushed inward. Nancy lost her balance and disappeared into a gaping hole below!

Helen screamed. "Nancy!"

Trembling with fright, Helen stepped into the closet and beamed her flashlight below. She could see a long flight of stone steps.

"Nancy! Nancy!" Helen called down.

A muffled answer came from below. Helen's heart gave a leap of relief. "Nancy's alive!" she told herself, then called, "Where are you?"

"I've found the secret passageway," came faintly to Helen's ears. "Come on down."

Helen did not hesitate. She wanted to be certain that Nancy was all right. Just as she started down the steps, the door began to close. Helen, in a panic that the girls might be trapped in some subterranean passageway, made a wild grab for the door. Holding it ajar, she removed the sweater she was wearing and wedged it into the opening.

Finding a rail on one side of the stone steps, Helen grasped it and hurried below. Nancy arose from the dank earthen floor to meet her.

"Are you sure you're all right?" Helen asked solicitously.

"I admit I got a good bang," Nancy replied, "but I feel fine now. Let's see where this passageway goes."

The flashlight had been thrown from her hand, but with the aid of Helen's light, she soon found it. Fortunately, it had not been damaged and she turned it on.

The passageway was very narrow and barely high enough for the girls to walk without bending over. The sides were built of crumbling brick and stone.

"This may tumble on us at any moment," Helen said worriedly.

"Oh, I don't believe so," Nancy answered. "It must have been here for a long time."

The subterranean corridor was unpleasantly damp and had an earthy smell. Moisture clung to the walls. They felt clammy and repulsive to the touch.

Presently the passageway began to twist and turn, as if its builders had found obstructions too difficult to dig through.

"Where do you think this leads?" Helen whispered.

"I don't know. I only hope we're not going in circles."

Presently the girls reached another set of stone steps not unlike the ones down which Nancy had tumbled. But these had solid stone sides. By their lights, the girls could see a door at the top with a heavy wooden bar across it.

"Shall we go up?" Helen asked.

Nancy was undecided what to do. The tunnel did not end here but yawned ahead in blackness. Should they follow it before trying to find out what was at the top of the stairs?

She voiced her thoughts aloud, but Helen urged that they climb the stairs. "I'll be frank with you. I'd like to get out of here."

Nancy acceded to her friend's wish and led the way up the steps.

Suddenly both girls froze in their tracks.

A man's voice from the far end of the tunnel commanded, "Stop! You can't go up there!"

CHAPTER XX

Nancy's Victory

THEIR initial fright over, both girls turned and beamed their flashlights toward the foot of the stone stairway. Below them stood a short, unshaven, pudgy man with watery blue eyes.

"You're the ghost!" Helen stammered.

"And you're Mr. Willie Wharton," Nancy added.

Astounded, the man blinked in the glaring lights, then said, "Ye-yes, I am. But how did you know?"

"You live in the old Riverview Manor," Helen went on, "and you've been stealing food and silver and jewelry from Twin Elms!"

"No, no. I'm not a thief!" Willie Wharton cried out. "I took some food and I've been trying to scare the old ladies, so they would sell their property. Sometimes I wore false faces, but I never took any jewelry or silver. Honest I didn't. It must have been Mr. Gomber."

Nancy and Helen were amazed—Willie Wharton, with little urging from them, was confessing more than they had dared to hope.

"Did you know that Nathan Gomber is a thief?" Nancy asked the man.

Wharton shook his head. "I know he's sharp— that's why he's going to get me more money for my property from the railroad."

"Mr. Wharton, did you sign the original contract of sale?" Nancy queried.

"Yes, I did, but Mr. Gomber said that if I disappeared for a while, he'd fix everything up so I'd get more money. He said he had a couple of other jobs which I could help him with. One of them was coming here to play ghost—it was a good place to disappear to. But I wish I had never seen Nathan Gomber or Riverview Manor or Twin Elms or had anything to do with ghosts."

"I'm glad to hear you say that," said Nancy. Then suddenly she asked, "Where's my father?"

Willie Wharton shifted his weight and looked about wildly. "I don't know, really I don't."

"But you kidnaped him in your car," the young sleuth prodded him. "We got a description of you from the taximan."

Several seconds went by before Willie Wharton answered. "I didn't know it was kidnaping. Mr. Gomber said your father was ill and that he was going to take him to a special doctor. He said Mr. Drew was coming on a train from Chicago and was going to meet Mr. Gomber on the road half-way between here and the station. But Gomber said he couldn't meet him—had other business to attend to. So I was to follow your father's taxi and bring him to Riverview Manor."

"Yes, yes, go on," Nancy urged, as Willie Wharton stopped speaking and covered his face with his hands.

"I didn't expect your father to be unconscious when I picked him up," Wharton went on. "Well, those men in the taxi put Mr. Drew in the back of my car and I brought him here. Mr. Gomber drove up from the other direction and said he would take over. He told me to come right here to Twin Elms and do some ghosting."

"And you have no idea where Mr. Gomber took my father?" Nancy asked, with a sinking feeling.

"Nope."

In a few words she pointed out Nathan Gomber's real character to Willie Wharton, hoping that if the man before her did know anything about Mr. Drew's whereabouts which he was not telling, he would confess. But from Wharton's emphatic answers and sincere offers to be of all the help he could in finding the missing lawyer, Nancy concluded that Wharton was not withholding any information.

"How did you find out about this passageway and the secret staircases?" Nancy questioned him.

"Gomber found an old notebook under a heap of rubbish in the attic of Riverview Manor," Wharton answered. "He said it told everything about the secret entrances to the two houses. The passageways, with openings on each floor, were built when the houses were. They were used by the original Turnbulls in bad weather to get from one building to the other. This stairway was for the servants. The other two stairways were for the family. One of these led to Mr. Turnbull's bedroom in this house. The notebook also said that he often secretly entertained government agents and sometimes he had to hurry them out of the parlor and hide them in the passageway when callers came."

"Where does this stairway lead?" Helen spoke up.

"To the attic of Twin Elms." Willie Wharton gave a little chuckle. "I know, Miss Drew, that you almost found the entrance. But the guys that built the place were pretty clever. Every opening has heavy double doors. When you poked that screw driver through the crack, you thought you were hitting another wall but it was really a door."

"Did you play the violin and turn on the radio —and make that thumping noise in the attic— and were you the one who laughed when we were up there?"

"Yes, and I moved the sofa to scare you and I even knew about the listening post. That's how I found out all your plans and could report them to Mr. Gomber."

Suddenly it occurred to Nancy that Nathan Gomber might appear on the scene at any moment. She must get Willie Wharton away and have him swear to his signature before he changed his mind!

"Mr. Wharton, would you please go ahead of us up this stairway and open the doors?" she asked. "And go into Twin Elms with us and talk to Mrs. Turnbull and Mrs. Hayes? I want you to tell them that you've been playing ghost but aren't going to any longer. Miss Flora has been so frightened that she's ill and in bed."

"I'm sorry about that," Willie Wharton replied. "Sure I'll go with you. I never want to see Nathan Gomber again!"

He went ahead of the girls and took down the heavy wooden bar from across the door. He swung it wide, pulled a metal ring in the back of the adjoining door, then quickly stepped downward. The narrow panel opening which Nancy had suspected of leading to the secret stairway now was pulled inward. There was barely room alongside it to go up the top steps and into the attic. To keep Gomber from becoming suspicious if he should arrive, Nancy asked Willie Wharton to close the secret door again.

"Helen," said Nancy, "will you please run downstairs ahead of Mr. Wharton and me and tell Miss Flora and Aunt Rosemary the good news."

She gave Helen a three-minute start, then she and Willie Wharton followed. The amazed women were delighted to have the mystery solved. But there was no time for celebration.

"Mr. Barradale is downstairs to see you, Nancy," Aunt Rosemary announced.

Nancy turned to Willie Wharton. "Will you come down with me, please?"

She introduced both herself and the missing property owner to Mr. Barradale, then went on, "Mr. Wharton says the signature on the contract of sale is his own."

"And you'll swear to that?" the lawyer asked, turning to Willie.

"I sure will. I don't want anything more to do with this underhanded business," Willie Wharton declared.

"I know where I can find a notary public right away," Nancy spoke up. "Do you want me to phone him, Mr. Barradale?" she asked.

"Please do. At once."

Nancy dashed to the telephone and dialed the number of Albert Watson on Tuttle Road. When he answered, she told him the urgency of the situation and he promised to come over at once. Mr. Watson arrived within five minutes, with his notary equipment. Mr. Barradale showed him the contract of sale containing Willie Wharton's name and signature. Attached to it was the certificate of acknowledgment.

Mr. Watson asked Willie Wharton to raise his right hand and swear that he was the person named in the contract of sale. After this was done, the notary public filled in the proper places on the certificate, signed it, stamped the paper, and affixed his seal.

"Well, this is really a wonderful job, Miss Drew," Mr. Barradale praised her.

Nancy smiled, but her happiness at having accomplished a task for her father was dampened by the fact that she still did not know where he was. Mr. Barradale and Willie Wharton also were extremely concerned.

"I'm going to call Captain Rossland and ask him to send some policemen out here at once," Nancy stated. "What better place for Mr. Gomber to hide my father than somewhere along that passageway? How far does it go, Mr. Wharton?"

"Mr. Gomber says it goes all the way to the river, but the end of it is completely stoned up now. I never went any farther than the stairways."

The young lawyer thought Nancy's idea a good one, because if Nathan Gomber should return to Riverview Manor and find that Willie was gone, he would try to escape.

The police promised to come at once. Nancy had just finished talking with Captain Rossland when Helen Corning called from the second floor.

"Nancy, can you come up here? Miss Flora insists upon seeing the hidden staircase."

The young sleuth decided that she would just about have time to do this before the arrival of the police. Excusing herself to Mr. Barradale, she ran up the stairs. Aunt Rosemary had put on a rose-colored dressing gown while attending her mother. To Nancy's amazement, Mrs. Turnbull was fully dressed and wore a white blouse with a high collar and a black skirt.

Nancy and Helen led the way to the attic. There, the girl detective, crouching on her knees, opened the secret door.

"And all these years I never knew it was here!" Miss Flora exclaimed.

"And I doubt that my father did or he would have mentioned it," Aunt Rosemary added.

Nancy closed the secret door and they all went downstairs. She could hear the front-door bell ringing and assumed that it was the police. She and Helen hurried below. Captain Rossland and another officer stood there. They said other men had surrounded Riverview Manor, hoping to catch Nathan Gomber if he did arrive there.

With Willie Wharton leading the way, the girls, Mr. Barradale, and the police trooped to the attic and went down the hidden staircase to the dank passageway below.

"I have a hunch from reading about old passage-ways that there may be one or more rooms off this tunnel," Nancy told Captain Rossland.

There were so many powerful flashlights in play now that the place was almost as bright as daylight. As the group moved along, they suddenly came to a short stairway. Willie Wharton explained that this led to an opening back of the sofa in the parlor. There was still another stone stairway which went up to Miss Flora's bedroom with an opening alongside the fireplace.

The searchers went on. Nancy, who was ahead of the others, discovered a padlocked iron door in the wall. Was it a dungeon? She had heard of such places being used for prisoners in Colonial times.

By this time Captain Rossland had caught up to her. "Do you think your father may be in there?" he asked.

"I'm terribly afraid so," said Nancy, shivering at the thought of what she might find.

The officer found that the lock was very rusty. Pulling from his pocket a penknife with various tool attachments, he soon had the door unlocked and flung it wide. He beamed his light into the blackness beyond. It was indeed a room without windows.

Suddenly Nancy cried out, "Dad!" and sprang ahead.

Lying on blankets on the floor, and covered with others, was Mr. Drew. He was murmuring faintly.

"He's alive!" Nancy exclaimed, kneeling down to pat his face and kiss him.

"He's been drugged," Captain Rossland observed. "I'd say Nathan Gomber has been giving your father just enough food to keep him alive and mixing sleeping powders in with it."

From his trousers pocket the officer brought out a small vial of restorative and held it to Mr. Drew's nose. In a few moments the lawyer shook his head, and a few seconds later, opened his eyes.

"Keep talking to your dad," the captain ordered Nancy.

"Dad! Wake up! You're all right! We've rescued you!"

Within a very short time Mr. Drew realized that his daughter was kneeling beside him. Reaching out his arms from beneath the blankets, he tried to hug her.

"We'll take him upstairs," said Captain Rossland. "Willie, open that secret entrance to the parlor."

"Glad to be of help." Wharton hurried ahead and up the short flight of steps.

In the meantime, the other three men lifted Mr. Drew and carried him along the passageway. By the time they reached the stairway, Willie

Wharton had opened the secret door behind the sofa in the parlor. Mr. Drew was placed on the couch. He blinked, looked around, and then said in astonishment:

"Willie Wharton! How did you get here? Nancy, tell me the whole story."

The lawyer's robust health and sturdy constitution had stood him in good stead. He recovered with amazing rapidity from his ordeal and listened in rapt attention as one after another of those in the room related the events of the past few days.

As the story ended, there was a knock on the front door and another police officer was admitted. He had come to report to Captain Rossland that not only had Nathan Gomber been captured outside of Riverview Manor, and all the loot recovered, but also that the final member of the group who had abducted Mr. Drew had been taken into custody. Gomber had admitted everything, even to having attempted to injure Nancy and her father with the truck at the River Heights' bridge project. He had tried to frighten Miss Flora into selling Twin Elms because he had planned to start a housing project on the two Turnbull properties.

"It's a real victory for you!" Nancy's father praised his daughter proudly.

The young sleuth smiled. Although she was glad it was all over, she could not help but look forward to another mystery to solve. One soon came her way when, quite accidentally, she found herself involved in *The Bungalow Mystery*.

Miss Flora and Aunt Rosemary had come downstairs to meet Mr. Drew. While they were talking to him, the police officer left, taking Willie Wharton with him as a prisoner. Mr. Barradale also said good-by. Nancy and Helen slipped out of the room and went to the kitchen.

"We'll prepare a super-duper lunch to celebrate this occasion!" said Helen happily.

"And we can make all the plans we want," Nancy replied with a grin. "There won't be anyone at the listening post!"

Match Wits with The Hardy Boys®!

Collect the Complete
Hardy Boys Mystery Stories®
by Franklin W. Dixon

Celebrate over 70 Years with the World's Greatest Super Sleuths!

Match Wits with Super Sleuth Nancy Drew!

Collect the Complete
Nancy Drew Mystery Stories®
by Carolyn Keene

Celebrate over 70 years with the World's Best Detective